Leveled Texts
for
Classic Fiction

Historical Fiction

Collected and Leveled by Christine Dugan

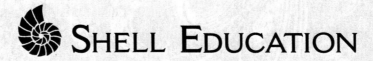

SHELL EDUCATION

Contributing Author

Wendy Conklin, M.S.

Publishing Credits

Dona Herweck Rice, *Editor-in-Chief*; Robin Erickson, *Production Director*; Lee Aucoin, *Creative Director*; Timothy J. Bradley, *Illustration Manager*; Sara Johnson, M.S.Ed., *Senior Editor*; Evelyn Garcia, *Associate Education Editor*; Grace Alba, *Designer*; Corinne Burton, M.A.Ed., *Publisher*

Image Credits

All images Shutterstock

Standards
© 2004 Mid-continent Research for Education and Learning (McREL)
© 2010 National Governors Association Center for Best Practices and Council of Chief State School Officers (CCSS)

Shell Education

5301 Oceanus Drive
Huntington Beach, CA 92649
http://www.shelleducation.com
ISBN 978-1-4258-0986-7
© 2013 Shell Educational Publishing, Inc.

Table of Contents

What Is Fiction?

Fiction is the work of imaginative narration. In other words, it is something that is made, as opposed to something that has happened or something that is discovered. It helps bring our imaginations to life, since it offers an escape into a world where everything happens for a reason—nothing is by chance. Fiction includes three main elements: plot (sequence), character, and setting (place).

Each event occurs in a logical order, and somehow, the conflict is resolved. Fiction promises a resolution in the end, and so the reader waits for resolution as the characters change, grow, and survive experiences. We are drawn to fiction because it is very close to the story of our lives. Fiction suggests that our own stories will have meaning and a resolution in the end. Perhaps that might be the reason why we love fiction—it delivers what it promises.

Fiction compels its readers to care about the characters whether they are loyal friends or conniving enemies. Readers dream about the characters and mourn their heartaches. Readers might feel that they know a fictional character's story intimately because he or she reminds them of a friend or family member. Additionally, the place described in the story might feel like a real place the reader has visited or would like to visit.

Fiction vs. Nonfiction

Fiction is literature that stems from the imagination and includes genres such as mystery, adventure, fairy tales, and fantasy. Fiction can include facts, but the story is not true in its entirety. Facts are often exaggerated or manipulated to suit an author's intent for the story. Realistic fiction uses plausible characters and storylines, but the people do not really exist and/ or the events narrated did not ever really take place. In addition, fiction is descriptive, elaborate, and designed to entertain. It allows readers to make their own interpretations based on the text.

Nonfiction includes a wide variety of writing styles that deal exclusively with real events, people, places, and things such as biographies, cookbooks, historical records, and scientific reports. Nonfiction is literature based on facts or perceived facts. In literature form, nonfiction deals with events that have actually taken place and relies on existing facts. Nonfiction writing is entirely fact-based. It states only enough to establish a fact or idea and is meant to be informative. Nonfiction is typically direct, clear, and simple in its message. Despite the differences, both fiction and nonfiction have a benefit and purpose for all readers.

The Importance of Using Fiction

Reading fiction has many benefits: It stimulates the imagination, promotes creative thinking, increases vocabulary, and improves writing skills. However, "students often hold negative attitudes about reading because of dull textbooks or being forced to read" (Bean 2000).

Fiction books can stimulate imagination. It is easy to get carried away with the character Percy Jackson as he battles the gods in *The Lightning Thief* (Riordan 2005). Readers can visualize what the author depicts. Researcher Keith Oatley (2009) states that fiction allows individuals to stimulate the minds of others in a sense of expanding on how characters might be feeling and what they might be thinking. When one reads fiction, one cannot help but visualize the nonexistent characters and places of the story. Lisa Zunshine (2006) has emphasized that fiction allows readers to engage in a theory-of-mind ability that helps them practice what the characters experience.

Since the work of fiction is indirect, it requires analysis if one is to get beyond the surface of the story. On the surface, one can view *Moby Dick* (Melville 1851) as an adventure story about a man hunting a whale. On closer examination and interpretation, the novel might be seen as a portrayal of good and evil. When a reader examines, interprets, and analyzes a work of fiction, he or she is promoting creative thinking. Creativity is a priceless commodity, as it facilitates problem solving, inventions, and creations of all kinds, and promotes personal satisfaction as well.

Reading fiction also helps readers build their vocabularies. Readers cannot help but learn a myriad of new words in Lemony Snicket's *A Series of Unfortunate Events* (1999). Word knowledge and reading comprehension go hand in hand. In fact, "vocabulary knowledge is one of the best predictors of reading achievement" (Richek 2005). Further, "vocabulary knowledge promotes reading fluency, boosts reading comprehension, improves academic achievement, and enhances thinking and communication" (Bromley 2004). Most researchers believe that students have the ability to add between 2,000 to 3,000 new words each school year, and by fifth grade, that number can be as high as 10,000 new words in their reading alone (Nagy and Anderson 1984). By exposing students to a variety of reading selections, educators can encourage students to promote the vocabulary growth that they need to be successful.

Finally, reading fictional text has a strong impact on students' ability as writers. According to Gay Su Pinnell (1988), "As children read and write, they make the connections that form their basic understandings about both....There is ample evidence to suggest that the processes are inseparable and that teachers should examine pedagogy in the light of these interrelationships." Many of the elements students encounter while reading fiction can transition into their writing abilities.

The Importance of Using Fiction *(cont.)*

Text Complexity

Text complexity refers to reading and comprehending various texts with increasing complexity as students progress through school and within their reading development. The Common Core State Standards (2010) state that "by the time they [students] complete the core, students must be able to read and comprehend independently and proficiently the kinds of complex texts commonly found in college and careers." In other words, by the time students complete high school, they must be able to read and comprehend highly complex texts, so students must consistently increase the level of complexity tackled at each grade level. Text complexity relies on the following combination of quantitative and qualitative factors:

Quantitative Factors	
Word Frequency	This is how often a particular word appears in the text. If an unfamiliar high-frequency word appears in a text, chances are the student will have a difficult time understanding the meaning of the text.
Sentence Length	Long sentences and sentences with embedded clauses require a lot from a young reader.
Word Length	This is the number of syllables in a word. Longer words are not by definition hard to read, but certainly can be for young readers.
Text Length	This refers to the number of words within the text passage.
Text Cohesion	This is the overall structure of the text. A high-cohesion text guides readers by signaling relationships among sentences through repetition and concrete language. A low-cohesion text does not have such support.

Qualitative Factors	
Level of Meaning or Purpose of Text	This refers to the objective and/or purpose for reading.
Structure	Texts that display low complexity are known for their simple structure. Texts that display high complexity are known for disruptions to predictable understandings.
Language Convention and Clarity	Texts that deviate from contemporary use of English tend to be more challenging to interpret.
Knowledge Demands	This refers to the background knowledge students are expected to have prior to reading a text. Texts that require students to possess a certain amount of previous knowledge are more complex than those that assume students have no prior knowledge.

(Adapted from the National Governors Association Center for Best Practices and Council of Chief State School Officers 2010)

The use of qualitative and quantitative measures to assess text complexity is demonstrated in the expectation that educators possess the ability to match the appropriate texts to the appropriate students. The passages in *Leveled Texts for Classic Fiction: Historical Fiction* vary in text complexity and will provide leveled versions of classic complex texts so that educators can scaffold students' comprehension of these texts. Educators can choose passages for students to read based on the reading level as well as the qualitative and quantitative complexity factors in order to find texts that are "just right" instructionally.

Genres of Fiction

There are many different fiction genres. The *Leveled Texts for Classic Fiction* series focuses on the following genres: adventure, fantasy and science fiction, mystery, historical fiction, mythology, humor, and Shakespeare.

Adventure stories transport readers to exotic places like deserted islands, treacherous mountains, and the high seas. This genre is dominated by fast-paced action. The plot often focuses on a hero's quest and features a posse that helps him or her achieve the goal. The story confronts the protagonist with events that disrupt his or her normal life and puts the character in danger. The story involves exploring and conquering the unknown accompanied by much physical action, excitement, and risk. The experience changes the protagonist in many ways.

The Importance of Using Fiction (cont.)

Fantasy and science fiction are closely related. Fantasy, like adventure, involves quests or journeys that the hero must undertake. Within fantasy, magic and the supernatural are central and are used to suggest universal truths. Events happen outside the laws that govern our universe. Science fiction also operates outside of the laws of physics but typically takes place in the future, space, another world, or an alternate dimension. Technology plays a strong role in this genre. Both science fiction and fantasy open up possibilities (such as living in outer space and talking to animals) because the boundaries of the real world cannot confine the story. Ideas are often expressed using symbols.

Mystery contains intriguing characters with suspenseful plots and can often feel very realistic. The story revolves around a problem or puzzle to solve: *Who did it? What is it? How did it happen?* Something is unknown, or a crime needs to be solved. Authors give readers clues to the solution in a mystery, but they also distract the reader by intentionally misleading them.

Historical fiction focuses on a time period from the past with the intent of offering insight into what it was like to live during that time. This genre incorporates historical research into the stories to make them feel believable. However, much of the story is fictionalized, whether it is conversations or characters. Often, these stories reveal that concerns from the past are still concerns. Historical fiction centers on historical events, periods, or figures.

Myths are collections of sacred stories from ancient societies. Myths are ways to explain questions about the creation of the world, the gods, and human life. For example, mythological stories often explain why natural events like storms or floods occur or how the world and living things came to be in existence. Myths can be filled with adventures conflict, between humans, and gods with extraordinary powers. These gods possess emotions and personality traits that are similar to humans.

Humor can include parody, joke books, spoofs, and twisted tales, among others. Humorous stories are written with the intent of being light-hearted and fun in order to make people laugh and to entertain. Often, these stories are written with satire and dry wit. Humorous stories also can have a very serious or dark side, but the ways in which the characters react and handle the situations make them humorous.

Shakespeare's plays can be classified in three genres: comedy, tragedy, and history. Shakespeare wrote his plays during the late 1500s and early 1600s, and performed many of them in the famous Globe Theater in London, England. Within each play is not just one coherent story but also a set of two or three stories that can be described as "plays within a play." His plays offer multiple perspectives and contradictions to make the stories rich and interesting. Shakespeare is noted for his ability to bring thoughts to life. He used his imagination to adapt stories, history, and other plays to entertain his audiences.

Elements of Fiction

The many common characteristics found throughout fiction are known as the elements of fiction. Among such elements are *point of view*, *character*, *setting*, and *plot*. *Leveled Texts for Classic Fiction* concentrates on setting, plot, and character, with an emphasis on language usage.

Language usage typically refers to the rules for making language. This series includes the following elements: *personification*, *hyperbole*, *alliteration*, *onomatopoeia*, *imagery*, *symbolism*, *metaphor*, and *word choice*. The table below provides a brief description of each.

Language Usage	Definition	Example
Personification	Giving human traits to nonhuman things	The chair moaned when she sat down on it.
Hyperbole	Extreme exaggeration	He was so hungry, he could eat a horse.
Alliteration	Repetition of the beginning consonant sounds	She sold seashells by the seashore.
Onomatopoeia	Forming a word from the sound it makes	Knock-knock, woof, bang, sizzle, hiss
Imagery	Language that creates a meaningful visual experience for the reader	His socks filled the room with a smell similar to a wet dog on a hot day.
Symbolism	Using objects to represent something else	A heart represents *love*.
Metaphor	Comparison of two unrelated things	My father is the rock of our family.
Word Choice	Words that an author uses to make the story memorable and to capture the reader's attention	In chapter two of *Holes* by Louis Sachar (2000), the author directly addresses the reader, saying, "The reader is probably asking…." The author predicts what the reader is wondering.

Elements of Fiction (cont.)

Setting is the *where* and *when* of a story's action. Understanding setting is important to the interpretation of the story. The setting takes readers to other times and places. Setting plays a large part in what makes a story enjoyable for the reader.

Plot forms the core of what the story is about and establishes the chain of events that unfolds in the story. Plot contains a character's motivation and the subsequent cause and effect of the character's actions. A plot diagram is an organizational tool that focuses on mapping out the events in a story. By mapping out the plot structure, students are able to visualize the key features of a story. The following is an example of a plot diagram:

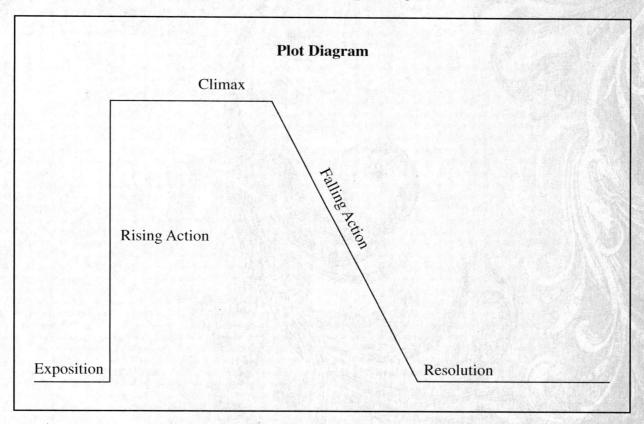

Plot Diagram

Climax

Rising Action

Falling Action

Exposition

Resolution

Characters are the people in the story. The protagonist is the main or leading character. He or she might be the narrator of the story. The antagonist is the force or character that acts against the protagonist. This antagonist is not always a person; it could be things such as weather, technology, or even a vehicle. Both the protagonist and antagonist can be considered dynamic, which means that they change or grow during the story as opposed to remaining static, or unchanging, characters. Readers engage with the text as they try to understand what motivates the characters to think and act as they do. Desires, values, and outside pressures all motivate characters' actions and help to determine the story's outcome.

A Closer Look at Historical Fiction

Historical fiction tells a story set in the past that does not conflict with historical records. Characters are portrayed realistically and the setting is authentic. The plot is supported by historical evidence and historical facts are sprinkled throughout the story. The story is foremost while the historical information is second to the story. This story might give a glimpse into everyday life at that time period. It might be about historical figures, or the characters might be unknowns who battle on the front lines or tell their stories of troubled times.

In this book you will find excerpts from works of historical fiction from classic fiction. The titles are as follows:

- *Our Little Celtic Cousin of Long Ago* by Evaleen Stein
- *The Store Boy* by Horatio Alger Jr.
- *The Rover Boys at School* by Edward Stratemeyer
- *The Prince and the Pauper* by Mark Twain
- *A Little Princess* by Frances Hodgson Burnett
- *Rainbow Valley* by Lucy Maud Montgomery
- *Little Women* by Louisa May Alcott
- *The Lords of the Wild* by Joseph A. Altsheler
- *Kidnapped* by Robert L. Stevenson
- *In the Days of the Guild* by Louise Lamprey
- *Anne of Green Gables* by Lucy Maud Montgomery
- *The Puritan Twins* by Lucy Fitch Perkins
- *The Red Badge of Courage* by Stephen Crane
- *The Secret Garden* by Frances Hodgson Burnett
- *The Guns of Bull Run* by Joseph A. Altsheler

A Closer Look at Historical Fiction *(cont.)*

Although there are many elements of fiction that can be studied in each passage of this book, the chart below outlines the strongest element portrayed in each passage.

Element of Fiction	Passage Title
Setting	• Excerpt from *Our Little Celtic Cousin of Long Ago* • Excerpt from *The Store Boy* • Excerpt from *The Rover Boys at School*
Character	• Excerpt from *The Prince and the Pauper* • Excerpt from *A Little Princess* • Excerpt from *Rainbow Valley* • Excerpt from *Little Women*
Plot	• Excerpt from *The Lords of the Wild* • Excerpt from *Kidnapped* • Excerpt from *In the Days of the Guild* • Excerpt from *Anne of Green Gables*
Language Usage	• Excerpt from *The Puritan Twins* • Excerpt from *The Red Badge of Courage* • Excerpt from *The Secret Garden* • Excerpt from *The Guns of Bull Run*

Leveled Texts to Differentiate Instruction

Today's classrooms contain diverse pools of learners. Above-level, on-level, below-level, and English language learners all come together to learn from one teacher in one classroom. The teacher is expected to meet their diverse needs. These students have different learning styles, come from different cultures, experience a variety of emotions, and have varied interests. And, they differ in academic readiness when it comes to reading. At times, the challenges teachers face can be overwhelming as they struggle to create learning environments that address the differences in their students while at the same time ensure that all students master the required grade-level objectives.

What is differentiation? Tomlinson and Imbau say, "Differentiation is simply a teacher attending to the learning needs of a particular student or small group of students, rather than teaching a class as though all individuals in it were basically alike" (2010). Any teacher who keeps learners at the forefront of his or her instruction can successfully provide differentiation. The effective teacher asks, "What am I going to do to shape instruction to meet the needs of all my learners?" One method or methodology will not reach all students.

Differentiation includes what is taught, how it is taught, and the products students create to show what they have learned. When differentiating curriculum, teachers become organizers of learning opportunities within the classroom environment. These opportunities are often referred to as *content*, *process*, and *product*.

- **Content:** Differentiating the content means to put more depth into the curriculum through organizing the curriculum concepts and structure of knowledge.

- **Process:** Differentiating the process requires using varied instructional techniques and materials to enhance student learning.

- **Product:** Cognitive development and students' abilities to express themselves improves when products are differentiated.

Leveled Texts to Differentiate Instruction (cont.)

Teachers should differentiate by content, process, and product according to students' differences. These differences include student *readiness*, *learning styles*, and *interests*.

- **Readiness:** If a learning experience aligns closely with students' previous skills and understanding of a topic, they will learn better.

- **Learning styles:** Teachers should create assignments that allow students to complete work according to their personal preferences and styles.

- **Interests:** If a topic sparks excitement in the learners, then students will become involved in learning and better remember what is taught.

Typically, reading teachers select different novels or texts that are leveled for their classrooms because only one book may either be too difficult or too easy for a particular group of students. One group of students will read one novel while another group reads another, and so on. What makes *Leveled Texts for Classic Fiction: Historical Fiction* unique is that all students, regardless of reading level, can read the same selection from a story and can participate in whole-class discussions about it. This is possible because each selection is leveled at four different reading levels to accommodate students' reading abilities. Regardless of the reading level, all of the selections present the same content. Teachers can then focus on the same content standard or objective for the whole class, but individual students can access the content at their particular instructional levels rather than their frustration level and avoid the frustration of a selection at too high or low a level.

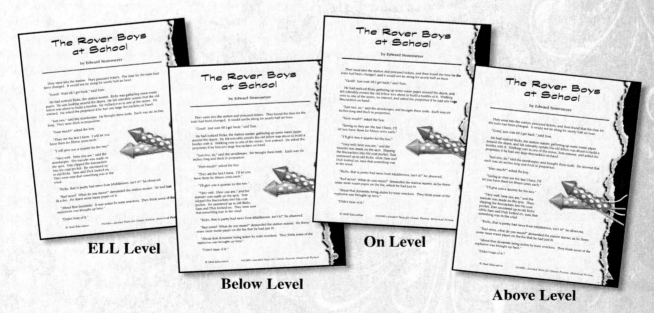

ELL Level

Below Level

On Level

Above Level

Leveled Texts to Differentiate Instruction *(cont.)*

Teachers should use the texts in this series to scaffold the content for their students. At the beginning of the year, students at the lowest reading levels may need focused teacher guidance. As the year progresses, teachers can begin giving students multiple levels of the same text to allow them to work independently at improving their comprehension. This means that each student will have a copy of the text at his or her independent reading level and at the instructional reading level. As students read the instructional-level texts, they can use the lower-leveled texts to better understand difficult vocabulary. By scaffolding the content in this way, teachers can support students as they move up through the reading levels and encourage them to work with texts that are closer to the grade level at which they will be tested.

A teacher does not need to draw attention to the fact that the texts are leveled. Nor should they hide it. Teachers who want students to read the text together can use homogeneous groups and distribute the texts after students join the groups. Or, teachers can distribute copies of the appropriate level to each student by copying the pages and separating them by each level.

Teaching Suggestions

Strategies for Higher-Order Thinking

Open-ended questions are a great way to infuse higher-order thinking skills into instruction. Open-ended questions have many appropriate answers and are exclusively dependent on the creativity of the student. Rarely do these questions have only one correct answer. It is up to the students to think and decide on their own what the answer should be. This is critical thinking at its very best. The following are some characteristics of open-ended questions:

- They ask students to *think* and *reflect*.
- They ask students to provide their *feelings* and *opinions*.
- They make students responsible for the *control* of the conversation.

There are many reasons to prefer open-ended over closed-ended questions. First, students must know the facts of the story to answer open-ended questions. Any higher-order question by necessity will encompass lower-order, fact-based questions. For a student to be able to answer a *what if* question (which is an example of an open-ended question), he or she must know the content of the story (which is a lower-level fact).

Open-ended questions also stimulate students to go beyond typical questions about a text. They spark real conversations about a text and are enriching. As a result, more students will be eager to participate in class discussions. In a more dynamic atmosphere, students will naturally make outside connections to the text, and there will be no need to force such connections.

Some students may at first be resistant to open-ended questions because they are afraid to think creatively. Years of looking for the one correct answer may make many students fear failure and embarrassment if they get the "wrong" answer. It will take time for these students to feel at ease with these questions. Model how to answer such questions. Keep encouraging students to answer them. Most importantly, be patient. The following are some examples of open-ended questions:

- Why do you think the author selected this setting?
- What are some explanations for the character's decisions?
- What are some lessons that this passage can teach us?
- How do the words set the mood or tone of this passage?

Teaching Suggestions *(cont.)*

Strategies for Higher-Order Thinking *(cont.)*

The tables below and on the following page are examples of open-ended questions and question stems that are specific to the elements of fiction covered in this series. Choose questions to challenge students to think more deeply about specific elements.

Setting
• In what ways did the setting…
• Describe the ways in which the author used setting to…
• What if the setting changed to…
• What are some possible explanations for selecting this setting?
• What would be a better setting for this story, and why is it better?
• Why did the author select this setting?
• What new element would you add to this setting to make it better?
• Explain several reasons why the characters fit well in this setting.
• Explain several reasons why the characters might fit better in a new setting.
• What makes this setting predictable or unpredictable?
• What setting would make the story more exciting? Explain.
• What setting would make the story dull? Explain.
• Why is the setting important to the story?

Character
• What is the likelihood that the character will…
• Form a hypothesis about what might happen to the character if…
• In what ways did the character show his/her thoughts by his/her actions?
• How might you have done this differently than the character?
• What are some possible explanations for the character's decisions about…
• Explain several reasons why the characters fit well in this setting.
• Explain several reasons why the characters don't fit well in this setting.
• What are some ways you would improve this character's description?
• Predict what the character will do next. Explain.
• What makes this character believable?
• For what reasons do you like or dislike this character?
• What makes this character memorable?
• What is the character thinking?

Teaching Suggestions *(cont.)*

Strategies for Higher-Order Thinking *(cont.)*

Plot

- How does this event affect…
- Predict the outcome…
- What other outcomes could have been possible, and why?
- What problems does this create?
- What is the likelihood…
- Propose a solution.
- Form a hypothesis.
- What is the theme of this story?
- What is the moral of this story?
- What lessons could this story teach us?
- How is this story similar to other stories you have read?
- How is this story similar to other movies you have watched?
- What sequel could result from this story?

Language Usage

- Describe the ways in which the author used language to…
- In what ways did language usage…
- What is the best description of…
- How would you have described this differently?
- What is a better way of describing this, and what makes it better?
- How can you improve upon the word selection…
- How can you improve upon the description of…
- What other words could be substituted for…
- What pictures do the words paint in your mind?
- How do the words set the mood or tone?
- Why would the author decide to use…
- What are some comparisons you could add to…
- In what ways could you add exaggeration to this sentence?

Teaching Suggestions *(cont.)*

Reading Strategies for Literature

The college and career readiness anchor standards within the Common Core State Standards in reading (National Governors Association Center for Best Practices and Council of Chief State School Officers 2010) include understanding key ideas and details, recognizing craft and structure, and being able to integrate knowledge and ideas. The following two pages offer practical strategies for achieving these standards using the texts found in this book.

Identifying Key Ideas and Details

- Have students work together to create talking tableaux based on parts of the text that infer information. A tableau is a freeze-frame where students are asked to pose and explain the scene from the text they are depicting. As students stand still, they take turns breaking away from the tableau to tell what is being inferred at that moment and how they know this. While this strategy is good for all students, it is a strong activity for **English language learners** because they have an opportunity for encoding and decoding with language and actions.

- Theme is the lesson that the story teaches its readers. It can be applied to everyone, not just the characters in the story. Have students identify the theme and write about what happens that results in their conclusions. Ask students to make connections as to how they can apply the theme to their lives. Allow **below-grade-level** writers to record this information, use graphic organizers for structure, or illustrate their answers in order to make the information more concrete for them.

- Have students draw a picture of the character during an important scene in the story, and use thought bubbles to show the character's secret thoughts based on specific details found in the text. This activity can benefit everyone, but it is very effective for **below-grade-level** writers and **English language learners**. Offering students an opportunity to draw their answers provides them with a creative method to communicate their ideas.

- Have students create before-and-after pictures that show how the characters change over the course of the story. Encourage **above-grade-level** students to examine characters' personality traits and how the characters' thoughts change. This activity encourages students to think about the rationale behind the personality traits they assigned to each character.

Teaching Suggestions (cont.)

Reading Strategies for Literature (cont.)

Understanding Craft and Structure

- Ask students to identify academic vocabulary in the texts and to practice using the words in a meet-and-greet activity in the classroom, walking around and having conversations using them. This gives **English language learners** an opportunity to practice language acquisition in an authentic way.

- Have students create mini-posters that display the figurative language used in the story. This strategy encourages **below-grade-level** students to show what they have learned.

- Allow students to work in pairs to draw sets of stairs on large paper, and then write how each part of the story builds on the previous part and fits together to provide the overall structure of the story. Homogeneously partner students so that **above-grade-level** students will challenge one another.

- Select at least two or three texts, and have students compare the point of view from which the different stories are narrated. Then, have students change the point of view (e.g., if the story is written in first person, have students rewrite a paragraph in third person). This is a challenging activity specifically suited for **on-grade-level** and **above-grade-level** students to stimulate higher-order thinking.

- Pose the following questions to students: What if the story is told from a different point of view? How does that change the story? Have students select another character's point of view and brainstorm lists of possible changes. This higher-order thinking activity is open-ended and effective for **on-level**, **above-level**, **below-level**, and **English language learners**.

Integrating Knowledge and Ideas

- Show students a section from a movie, a play, or a reader's theater about the story. Have students use graphic organizers to compare and contrast parts of the text with scenes from one of these other sources. Such visual displays support comprehension for **below-level** and **English language learners**.

- Have students locate several illustrations in the text, and then rate the illustrations based on their effective visuals. This higher-order thinking activity is open-ended and is great for **on-level**, **below-level**, **above-level**, and **English language learners**.

- Let students create playlists of at least five songs to go with the mood and tone of the story. Then instruct students to give an explanation for each chosen song. Musically inclined students tend to do very well with this type of activity. It also gives a reason for writing, which can engage **below-grade-level** writers.

- Have students partner up to create talk show segments that discuss similar themes found in the story. Each segment should last between one and two minutes and can be performed live or taped. Encourage students to use visuals, props, and other tools to make it real. Be sure to homogeneously group students for this activity and aid your **below-level** students so they can be successful. This activity allows for **all students** to bring their creative ideas to the table and positively contribute to the end result.

Teaching Suggestions (cont.)

Fiction as a Model for Writing

It is only natural that reading and writing go hand in hand in students' literacy development. Both are important for functioning in the real world as adults. Established pieces of fiction, like the ones in this book, serve as models for how to write effectively. After students read the texts in this book, take time for writing instruction. Below are some ideas for writing mini-lessons that can be taught using the texts from this book as writing exemplars.

How to Begin Writing a Story

Instead of beginning a story with 'Once upon a time' or 'Long, long ago,' teach students to mimic the styles of well-known authors. As students begin writing projects, show them a variety of first sentences or paragraphs written by different authors. Discuss how these selections are unique. Encourage students to change or adapt the types of beginnings found in the models to make their own story hooks.

Using Good Word Choice

Good word choice can make a significant difference in writing. Help students paint vivid word pictures by showing them examples within the passages found in this book. Instead of writing *I live in a beautiful house,* students can write *I live in a yellow-framed house with black shutters and white pillars that support the wraparound porch.* Encourage students to understand that writing is enriched with sensory descriptions that include what the characters smell, hear, taste, touch, and see. Make students aware of setting the emotional tone in their stories. For example, *In an instant, the hair on the back of his neck stood up, the door creaked open, and a hand reached through.* This example sets a scary mood. Hyperbole is also a great tool to use for effect in stories.

Character Names Can Have Meaning

Students can use names to indicate clues about their characters' personalities. Mrs. Strict could be a teacher, Dr. Molar could be a dentist, and Butch could be the class bully. Remind students that the dialogue between their characters should be real, not forced. Students should think about how people really talk and write dialogue using jargon and colorful words, for example, *"Hey you little twerp, come back here!" yelled Brutus.*

How to Use This Book

Classroom Management for Leveled Texts

Determining your students' instructional reading levels is the first step in the process of effectively managing the leveled-text passages. It is important to assess their reading abilities often so they do not get stuck on one level. Below are suggested ways to use this resource, as well as other resources available to you, to determine students' reading levels.

Running records: While your class is doing independent work, pull your below-grade-level students aside one at a time. Have them individually read aloud the lowest level of a text (the star level) as you record any errors they make on your own copy of the text. Assess their accuracy and fluency, mark the words they say incorrectly, and listen for fluent reading. Use your judgment to determine whether students seem frustrated as they read. If students read accurately and fluently and comprehend the material, move them up to the next level and repeat the process. Following the reading, ask comprehension questions to assess their understanding of the material. As a general guideline, students reading below 90 percent accuracy are likely to feel frustrated as they read. A variety of other published reading assessment tools are available to assess students' reading levels with the running-records format.

Refer to other resources: Another way to determine instructional reading levels is to check your students' Individualized Education Plans; ask the school's language development specialists and/or special education teachers; or review test scores. All of these resources can provide the additional information needed to determine students' reading levels.

How to Use This Book (cont.)

Distributing the Texts

Some teachers wonder about how to distribute the different-leveled texts within the classroom. They worry that students will feel insulted or insecure if they do not get the same material as their neighbors. Prior to distributing the texts, make sure that the classroom environment is one in which all students learn at their individual instructional levels. It is important to make this clear. Otherwise, students may constantly ask why their work is different from another student's work. Simply state that students will not be working on the same assignment every day and that their work may slightly vary to resolve students' curiosity. In this approach, distribution of the texts can be very open and causal, just like passing out any other assignment.

Teachers who would rather not have students aware of the differences in the texts can try the suggestions below:

- Make a pile in your hands from star to triangle. Put your finger between the circle and square levels. As you approach each student, pull from the top (star), above your finger (circle), below your finger (square), or the bottom (triangle), depending on each student's level. If you do not hesitate too much in front of each desk, students will probably not notice.

- Begin the class period with an opening activity. Put the texts in different places around the room. As students work quietly, circulate and direct students to the right locations for retrieving the texts you want them to use.

- Organize the texts in small piles by seating arrangement so that when you arrive at a group of desks, you will have only the levels you need.

How to Use This Book (cont.)

Components of the Product

Each passage is derived from classic literary selections. Classics expose readers to cultural heritage or the literature of a culture. Classics improve understanding of the past and, in turn, understanding of the present. These selections from the past explain how we got to where we are today.

The Levels

There are 15 passages in this book, each from a different work of classic fiction. Each passage is leveled to four different reading levels. The images and fonts used for each level within a topic look the same.

Behind each page number, you will see a shape. These shapes indicate the reading levels of each piece so that you can make sure students are working with the correct texts. The chart on the following page provides specific levels of each text.

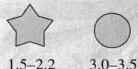

1.5–2.2   3.0–3.5

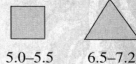

5.0–5.5   6.5–7.2

Leveling Process

The texts in this series are excerpts from classic pieces of literature. A reading specialist has reviewed each excerpt and leveled each one to create four distinct reading passages with unique levels.

Elements of Fiction Question

Each text includes one comprehension question that directs the students to think about the chosen element of fiction for that passage. These questions are written at the appropriate reading level to allow all students to successfully participate in a whole-class discussion. These questions are open-ended and designed to stimulate higher-order thinking.

Digital Resource CD

The Digital Resource CD allows for easy access to all the reading passages in this book. Electronic PDF files as well as word files are included on the CD.

Common Core State Standards

The texts in this book are aligned to the Common Core State Standards (CCSS). The standards correlation can be found on pages 28–29.

How to Use This Book (cont.)

	ELL Level	Below Level	On level	Above level
Setting Passages	⭐ 1.5–2.2	⬤ 3.0–3.5	⬛ 5.0–5.5	🔺 6.5–7.2
Our Little Celtic Cousin of Long Ago	2.2	3.5	5.0	6.7*
The Store Boy	2.2	3.5	5.5*	6.6
The Rover Boys at School	2.1	3.2	5.1*	6.7
Character Passages				
The Prince and the Pauper	2.2	3.5	5.3*	6.5
A Little Princess	2.2	3.5	5.5	6.6*
Rainbow Valley	2.2	3.4	5.0*	6.6
Little Women	1.5	3.5*	5.0	6.7
Plot Passages				
The Lords of the Wild	2.2	3.4	5.3*	6.5
Kidnapped	2.2	3.0	5.5*	7.2
In the Days of the Guild	2.2	3.4	5.0	6.6*
Anne of Green Gables	2.2	3.4	5.0	7.1*
Language Usage Passages				
The Puritan Twins	2.2	3.5	5.0	6.5*
The Red Badge of Courage	2.2	3.5	5.2*	6.5
The Secret Garden	1.9	3.2	5.0	6.5*
The Guns of Bull Run	2.2	3.5	5.0	7.1*

* The passages with an asterisk indicate the reading passage from the original work of fiction.

Correlations to Standards

Shell Education is committed to producing educational materials that are research and standards based. In this effort, we have correlated all our products to the academic standards of all 50 United States, the District of Columbia, the Department of Defense Dependent Schools, and all Canadian provinces.

How to Find Standards Correlations

To print a customized correlations report of this product for your state, visit our website at **http://www.shelleducation.com** and follow the on-screen directions. If you require assistance in printing correlations reports, please contact Customer Service at 1-800-858-7339.

Purpose and Intent of Standards

Legislation mandates that all states adopt academic standards that identify the skills students will learn in kindergarten through grade twelve. Many states also have standards for pre-K. This same legislation sets requirements to ensure the standards are detailed and comprehensive.

Standards are designed to focus instruction and guide adoption of curricula. Standards are statements that describe the criteria necessary for students to meet specific academic goals. They define the knowledge, skills, and content students should acquire at each level. Standards are also used to develop standardized tests to evaluate students' academic progress.

Teachers are required to demonstrate how their lessons meet state standards. State standards are used in the development of all our products, so educators can be assured they meet the academic requirements of each state.

McREL Compendium

We use the Mid-continent Research for Education and Learning (McREL) Compendium to create standards correlations. Each year, McREL analyzes state standards and revises the compendium. By following this procedure, McREL is able to produce a general compilation of national standards. Each lesson in this product is based on one or more McREL standards. The chart on the following pages lists each standard taught in this product and the page numbers for the corresponding lessons.

TESOL Standards

The lessons in this book promote English language development for English language learners. The standards listed on the following pages support the language objectives presented throughout the lessons.

Common Core State Standards

The texts in this book are aligned to the Common Core State Standards (CCSS). The standards correlation can be found on pages 28–29.

Correlations to Standards *(cont.)*

Correlation to Common Core State Standards

The passages in this book are aligned to the Common Core State Standards (CCSS). Students who meet these standards develop the skills in reading that are the foundation for any creative and purposeful expression in language.

Grade(s)	Standard
3	RL.3.10—By the end of year, independently and proficiently read and comprehend literature, including stories, dramas, and poetry, at the high end of the grades 2–3 text-complexity band
4–5	RL.4.10–5.10—By the end of the year, proficiently read and comprehend literature, including stories, dramas, and poetry, in the grades 4–5 text-complexity band, with scaffolding as needed at the high end of the range
6–8	RL.6.10–8.10—By the end of the year, proficiently read and comprehend literature, including stories, dramas, and poems, in the grades 6–8 text-complexity band, with scaffolding as needed at the high end of the range.

As outlined by the Common Core State Standards, teachers are "free to provide students with whatever tools and knowledge their professional judgment and experience identify as most helpful for meeting the goals set out in the standards." Bearing this in mind, teachers are encouraged to use the recommendations indicated in the chart below in order to meet additional CCSS Reading Standards that require further instruction.

Standard	Additional Instruction
RL.3.1–5.1— Key Ideas and Details	• Ask and answer questions to demonstrate understanding of a text. • Refer to details and examples in a text. • Quote accurately from a text when explaining what the text says.
RL.3.2–5.2— Key Ideas and Details	• Recount stories to determine the central message, lesson, or moral and explain how it is conveyed. • Determine a theme of a story from details in the text.
RL.3.3–5.3— Key Ideas and Details	• Describe in depth a character, setting, or event in a story.
RL.6.1–8.1— Key Ideas and Details	• Cite textual evidence to support analysis of what the text says.
RL.6.2–8.2— Key Ideas and Details	• Determine a theme or central idea of a text and analyze its development over the course of the text.
RL.6.3–8.3— Key Ideas and Details	• Analyze how particular elements of a story or drama interact.

Correlations to Standards *(cont.)*

Correlation to Common Core State Standards *(cont.)*

Standard	Additional Instruction *(cont.)*
RL.3.4–8.4— Craft and Structure	• Determine the meaning of words and phrases as they are used in the text.
RL.3.5–5.5— Craft and Structure	• Refer to parts of stories when writing or speaking about a text. • Explain the overall structure of a story.
RL.3.6–8.6— Craft and Structure	• Distinguish and describe point of view within the story.
RL.6.5–8.5— Craft and Structure	• Analyze and compare and contrast the overall structure of a story.
RL.3.7–5.7— Integration of Knowledge and Ideas	• Explain how specific aspects of a text's illustrations contribute to what is conveyed by the words in a story.
RL.3.9–8.9— Integration of Knowledge and Ideas	• Compare and contrast the themes, settings, and plots of stories.

Correlation to McREL Standards

Standard	Page(s)
5.1—Previews text (3–5)	all
5.1—Establishes and adjusts purposes for reading (6–8)	all
5.2—Establishes and adjusts purposes for reading (3–5)	all
5.3—Makes, confirms, and revises simple predictions about what will be found in a text (3–5)	all
5.3—Uses a variety of strategies to extend reading vocabulary (6–8)	all
5.4—Uses specific strategies to clear up confusing parts of a text (6–8)	all
5.5—Use a variety of context clues to decode unknown words (3–5)	all
5.5—Understands specific devices an author uses to accomplish his or her purpose (6–8)	all
5.6—Reflects on what has been learned after reading and formulates ideas, opinions, and personal responses to texts (6–8)	all

Correlation to Standards *(cont.)*

Correlation to McREL Standards *(cont.)*

Standard	Page(s)
5.7—Understands level-appropriate reading vocabulary (3–5)	all
5.8—Monitors own reading strategies and makes modifications as needed (3–5)	all
5.10—Understands the author's purpose or point of view (3–5)	all
6.1—Reads a variety of literary passages and texts (3–5, 6–8)	all
6.2—Knows the defining characteristics and structural elements of a variety of literary genres (3–5, 6–8)	all
6.3—Understands the basic concept of plot (3–5)	all
6.3—Understands complex elements of plot development (6–8)	all
6.4—Understands similarities and differences within and among literary works from various genres and cultures (3–5)	all
6.4—Understands elements of character development (6–8)	all
6.5—Understands elements of character development in literary works (3–5)	all
6.7—Understands the ways in which language is used in literary texts (3–5)	all

Correlation to TESOL Standards

Standard	Page(s)
2.1—Students will use English to interact in the classroom	all
2.2—Students will use English to obtain, process, construct, and provide subject matter information in spoken and written form	all
2.3—Students will use appropriate learning strategies to construct and apply academic knowledge	all

Our Little Celtic Cousin of Long Ago

by Evaleen Stein

The boys were just starting off together. A sudden shouting arose.

"Look over there!" cried Ferdiad. "I believe they are beginning to course the hounds!"

Both lads ran across a space of green grass. There was a low, wattled fence. It enclosed a large oval racecourse. People were gathered about it. They were talking excitedly. They watched a dozen or more large wolf hounds. The dogs were doing lively capers. Several men held the dogs in leash. They used long leather thongs. The dogs were straining. They pulled impatiently at their collars. Then the signal was given. They were unleashed. "Br-rh-rh-rh-rh-rh!!" Off they darted. Their noses were pointing straight ahead. Their long legs and powerful bodies bounded past so swiftly. Neither Ferdiad nor Conn could make out one from another.

It took a few moments. Then the fastest began to sweep ahead. Conn cried out excitedly. "Look! Look! It is the big light-brown one. That is the one I picked out. He is leading!"

"Not now!" called back Ferdiad. They hurried along the fence. They followed the racing dogs with their eyes. "No! Now it is the one with the white tip to his tail!"

"Whew!" shouted Conn. There was a deep roar. The baying pack swept past again. "Look at that bright blue one. He was way behind. He is leading them all now!"

The panting hounds came around. They were on the last quarter of the track. It was the bright blue one that leaped first. He ran across. He passed the streak of white lime that marked the goal. The bystanders shouted. They clapped hands. The tired dogs were led off.

"Whose hound won? Do you know?" asked Conn of Ferdiad.

"I heard he belonged to Prince Cormac of Cromarty," answered Ferdiad. "The prize is an enameled dog collar. He also gets a leather leash trimmed with silver. When will the high king give it to him?"

"Not till the end of the fair," said a tall man. He was standing near. "The high king is not here yet. He is coming tomorrow. There will be games. There will be chariot races. There is also the poets' and storytellers' contest."

"That hound race was good," said Conn. The boys turned away. "I never thought the blue one would win! He was such a handsome color. I suppose Prince Cormac must have had him specially dyed. He did it for the fair."

"I have a green hound at home that is just as handsome," said Ferdiad. "My foster mother says she will color the next wool she spins. Then maybe she will have enough red left to dye another hound."

The Celts thought oddly colored animals to be very pretty. Women dyed the yarn that they all spun for themselves. Then they often emptied what was left in their dye-pots over the family pets. A purple cat or a blue or red dog was no uncommon sight.

Element Focus: Setting

What is a possible explanation for the author selecting this setting?

Excerpt from

Our Little Celtic Cousin of Long Ago

by Evaleen Stein

The boys were just starting off together when a sudden shouting arose.

"O, look over there!" cried Ferdiad, "I believe they are beginning to course the hounds!"

Both lads ran across a space of green grass. A low, wattled fence enclosed a large oval racecourse. People were gathered about it. They were talking excitedly. They watched the lively capers of a dozen or more large wolf hounds. Several men held the dogs in leash by long leather thongs. The dogs were straining impatiently at their collars. Then the signal was given. They were unleashed. "Br-rh-rh-rh-rh-rh!!" Off they darted. Their noses were pointing straight ahead. Their long legs and powerful bodies bounded past so swiftly. Neither Ferdiad nor Conn could make out one from another.

But in a few moments, the fastest began to sweep ahead. Conn cried out excitedly, "Look! Look! That big light-brown one I picked out is leading!"

"Not now!" called back Ferdiad. They hurried along the fence. They followed the racing dogs with their eyes. "No! Now it is the one with the white tip to his tail!"

"Whew!" shouted Conn. With a deep roar, the baying pack swept past again. "That bright blue one that was way behind is leading them all now!"

Sure enough, when the panting hounds came around the last quarter of the track, it was the bright blue one that leaped first across the streak of white lime that marked the goal. There was a great shouting and clapping of hands by the bystanders. The tired dogs were led off.

"Whose hound was it that won? Do you know?" asked Conn of Ferdiad.

"I heard a man say he belonged to Prince Cormac of Cromarty," answered Ferdiad. "The prize is an enameled dog collar and a leather leash trimmed with silver. I wonder when the high king will give it to him?"

"Not till the end of the fair, boy," said a tall man standing near. "The high king is not here yet. He is coming tomorrow. There will be games and chariot races. There is also the poets' and storytellers' contest."

"Well," said Conn as the boys turned away, "that hound race was good. I never thought the blue one would win! He was such a handsome color. I suppose Prince Cormac must have had him specially dyed for the fair."

"I dare say," said Ferdiad, "but I have a green hound at home that is just as handsome. My foster mother says when she colors the next wool she spins, maybe she will have enough red left to dye another hound."

For the Celts thought oddly colored animals to be very pretty. When women dyed the yarn that they all spun for themselves, they often emptied what was left in the dye-pots over the family pets. So a purple cat or a blue or red dog was no uncommon sight.

Element Focus: Setting

What other events are mentioned that
will also happen in this setting?

#50986—*Leveled Texts for Classic Fiction: Historical Fiction*   © *Shell Education*

Our Little Celtic Cousin of Long Ago

by Evaleen Stein

The boys were just starting off together when a sudden shouting arose.

"O, look over there!" cried Ferdiad, "I believe they are beginning to course the hounds!"

Both lads ran across a space of green grass. A low, wattled fence enclosed a large oval racecourse. People were gathered about it talking excitedly. They watched the lively capers of a dozen or more large wolf hounds that several men held in leash by long leather thongs. The dogs were straining impatiently at their collars. The moment the signal was given, they were unleashed, "Br-rh-rh-rh-rh-rh!" off they darted. Their noses were pointing straight ahead and their long legs and powerful bodies bounded past so swiftly that neither Ferdiad nor Conn could make out one from another.

But in a few moments, the fastest began to sweep ahead, and Conn cried out excitedly, "Look! Look! That big light-brown one I picked out is leading!"

"Not now!" called back Ferdiad. They hurried along the fence following the racing dogs with their eyes. "No! Now it's the one with the white tip to his tail!"

"Whew!" shouted Conn, as "Br-rh-rh-rh-rh-rh!" with a deep roar the baying pack swept past again, "If there isn't that bright blue one that was way behind leading them all now!"

And, sure enough, when the panting hounds came around the last quarter of the track, it was the bright blue one that leaped first across the streak of white lime that marked the goal. There was a great shouting and clapping of hands by the bystanders as the tired dogs were led off.

"Whose hound was it that won? Do you know?" asked Conn of Ferdiad.

"I heard a man say he belonged to Prince Cormac of Cromarty," answered Ferdiad. "They say the prize is an enameled dog collar and a leather leash trimmed with silver. I wonder when the high king will give it to him?"

"Not till the end of the fair, boy," said a tall man standing near. "The high king isn't here yet. He is coming tomorrow, and there will be games and chariot races. Last of all, the poets' and storytellers' contest."

"Well," said Conn as the boys turned away, "that hound race was good. But I never thought the blue one would win! He was such a handsome color. I suppose Prince Cormac must have had him specially dyed for the fair."

"I dare say," said Ferdiad, "but I have a green hound at home that is just as handsome, and my foster mother says when she colors the next wool she spins, maybe she will have enough red left to dye another hound."

For the Celts thought oddly colored animals to be very pretty, and when women dyed the yarn that they all spun for themselves, they often emptied what was left in their dye-pots over the family pets. So a purple cat or a blue or red dog was no uncommon sight.

Element Focus: Setting

Why is the setting important to the story?

Excerpt from

Our Little Celtic Cousin of Long Ago

by Evaleen Stein

The boys were just starting off together when a sudden shouting arose.

"O, look over there!" cried Ferdiad, "I believe they are beginning to course the hounds!"

Both lads ran across a space of green grass to where a low wattled fence enclosed a large oval race-course. People were gathered about it talking excitedly as they watched the lively capers of a dozen or more large wolf hounds that several men held in leash by long leather thongs. The dogs were straining impatiently at their collars, and the moment the signal was given and they were unleashed, "Br-rh-rh-rh-rh-rh!!" off they darted, their noses pointing straight ahead and their long legs and powerful bodies bounding past so swiftly that neither Ferdiad nor Conn could make out one from another.

But in a few moments the fastest began to sweep ahead, and Conn cried out excitedly, "Look! Look! That big light brown one I picked out is leading!"

"Not now!" called back Ferdiad, as they hurried along the fence following the racing dogs with their eyes. "No! now it's the one with the white tip to his tail!"

"Whew!" shouted Conn, as "Br-rh-rh-rh-rh-rh!" with a deep roar the baying pack swept past again, "If there isn't that bright blue one that was 'way behind leading them all now!"

And, sure enough, when the panting hounds came around the last quarter of the track it was the bright blue that leaped first across the streak of white lime that marked the goal. There was a great shouting and clapping of hands by the bystanders as the tired dogs were led off.

"Whose hound was it that won? Do you know?" asked Conn of Ferdiad.

"I heard a man say he belonged to Prince Cormac of Cromarty," answered Ferdiad. "They say the prize is an enameled dog-collar and a leather leash trimmed with silver. I wonder when the high king will give it to him?"

"Not till the end of the fair, boy," said a tall man standing near. "The high king isn't here yet but is coming tomorrow, and there will be games and chariot races yet, and, last of all, the poets' and storytellers' contest."

"Well," said Conn as the boys turned away, "that hound race was good,—but I never thought the blue one would win! He was such a handsome color I suppose Prince Cormac must have had him specially dyed for the fair."

"I dare say," said Ferdiad, "but I have a green hound at home that is just as handsome, and my foster mother says when she colors the next wool she spins maybe she will have enough red left to dye another one."

For the Celts thought oddly colored animals very pretty, and women when they dyed the yarn which they all spun for themselves often emptied what was left in their dye-pots over the family pets. So a purple cat or blue or red dog was no uncommon sight.

Element Focus: Setting

What makes this setting predictable or unpredictable?

Excerpt from

The Store Boy

by Horatio Alger Jr.

Ben Barclay left the tramp. He lost no time. He drove to the grocery store. This is where he worked. It was a large country store. The store did not sell groceries alone. It had supplies of dry goods. It had boots and shoes. It had the leading articles required in the community. There were two other clerks. One was the son of Simon Crawford and another was his nephew. Crawford was the store owner.

"Did you collect any money?" asked Simon. He was standing at the door.

"Yes, sir. I collected twenty-five dollars. I almost lost it on the way home."

"How was that? I hope you were not careless."

"No. Except in taking a stranger as a passenger. We got to the woods a mile back. He asked me for all the money I had."

"A highwayman? Near Pentonville!" exclaimed Simon Crawford. "What was he like?"

"A regular tramp."

"Yet you say you have the money. How did you manage to keep it from him?"

Ben detailed the plan that he used.

"You did well," said the storekeeper. "I must give you a dollar for the one you sacrificed."

"Sir, it was bad money. I could not have passed it."

"That does not matter. You are entitled to some reward. You showed courage and quick wit. Here is a dollar. There is a show at the Town Hall tonight, isn't there?"

"Yes, sir. Prof. Harrington is a magician," said Ben eagerly.

"At what time?"

"At eight o'clock."

"You may leave the store at half-past seven. That will give you enough time to get there."

"Thank you, sir. I wanted to go. Yet I did not like to ask for the evening off."

"You have earned it. Here is the dollar." He handed the money to his young clerk. Ben took it.

A show may be common to people in the city. Yet in a country village, it is an event. Pentonville was small. It did not have any regular place of amusement. Its citizens depended on traveling performers. Such performers came from time to time. It had been a long time since there had been any such entertainment. So, Prof. Harrington was the more likely to be well attended. Ben liked to have fun like boys of his age. He had been sad to stay in the store till nine o'clock. Then he would miss out. Now, there was an opportunity.

"I am glad I met the tramp," he said to himself. "He has brought me luck."

Element Focus: Setting

What is different between
life in the country and in the city?

Excerpt from

The Store Boy

by Horatio Alger Jr.

Ben Barclay took leave of the tramp. He lost no time. He drove to the grocery store. This is where he was employed. It was a large country store. The store was not devoted to groceries alone. It had supplies of dry goods, boots, and shoes. It had the leading articles required in the community. There were two other clerks besides Ben. One was the son, another the nephew of Simon Crawford. Crawford was the proprietor.

"Did you collect any money, Ben?" asked Simon. He chanced to be standing at the door when our hero drove up.

"Yes, sir. I collected twenty-five dollars. I came near losing it on the way home."

"How was that? I hope you were not careless."

"No. Except in taking a stranger as a passenger. We got to that piece of woods a mile back. He asked me for all the money I had."

"A highwayman? And so near Pentonville!" exclaimed Simon Crawford. "What was he like?"

"A regular tramp."

"Yet you say you have the money. How did you manage to keep it from him?"

Ben detailed the plan that he used.

"You did well," said the storekeeper approvingly. "I must give you a dollar for the one you sacrificed."

"Sir, it was bad money. I could not have passed it."

"That does not matter. You are entitled to some reward for the courage and quick wit you displayed. Here is a dollar. There is an entertainment at the Town Hall this evening, isn't there?"

"Yes, sir. Prof. Harrington, the magician, gives an entertainment," said Ben eagerly.

"At what time does it commence?"

"At eight o'clock."

"You may leave the store at half-past seven. That will give you enough time to get there."

"Thank you, sir. I wanted to go to the entertainment. Yet I did not like to ask for the evening off."

"You have earned it. Here is the dollar." He handed the money to his young clerk. Ben received it gratefully.

A magical entertainment may be a very common affair to my young readers in the city. Yet in a country village, it is an event. Pentonville was too small to have any regular place of amusement. Its citizens had to depend upon traveling performers. Such performers engaged the Town Hall from time to time. Some time had elapsed since there had been any such entertainment. So, Prof. Harrington was the more likely to be well patronized. Ben had the love of amusement common to boys of his age. He had been regretting the necessity of remaining in the store till nine o'clock. Then, he would lose out his chance at amusement. As we have seen, an opportunity suddenly offered.

"I am glad I met the tramp," he said to himself. "He has brought me luck."

Element Focus: Setting

How is this large country store different
from stores in big cities?

Excerpt from

The Store Boy

by Horatio Alger Jr.

Ben Barclay, after taking leave of the tramp, lost no time in driving to the grocery store where he was employed. It was a large country store, devoted not to groceries alone, but supplies of dry-goods, boots and shoes, and the leading articles required in the community. There were two other clerks besides Ben, one the son, another the nephew, of Simon Crawford, the proprietor.

"Did you collect any money, Ben?" asked Simon, who chanced to be standing at the door when our hero drove up.

"Yes, sir; I collected twenty-five dollars, but came near losing it on the way home."

"How was that? I hope you were not careless."

"No, except in taking a stranger as a passenger. When we got to that piece of woods a mile back, he asked me for all the money I had."

"A highwayman, and so near Pentonville!" exclaimed Simon Crawford. "What was he like?"

"A regular tramp."

"Yet you say you have the money. How did you manage to keep it from him?"

Ben detailed the stratagem of which he made use.

"You did well," said the storekeeper approvingly. "I must give you a dollar for the one you sacrificed."

"But sir, it was bad money. I couldn't have passed it."

"That does not matter. You are entitled to some reward for the courage and quick wit you displayed. Here is a dollar, and, let me see, there is an entertainment at the Town Hall this evening, isn't there?"

"Yes, sir. Prof. Harrington, the magician, gives an entertainment," said Ben eagerly.

"At what time does it commence?"

"At eight o'clock."

"You may leave the store at half-past seven. That will give you enough time to get there."

"Thank you, sir. I wanted to go to the entertainment, but did not like to ask for the evening."

"You have earned it. Here is the dollar," and Mr. Crawford handed the money to his young clerk, who received it gratefully.

A magical entertainment may be a very common affair to my young readers in the city, but in a country village it is an event. Pentonville was too small to have any regular place of amusement, and its citizens were obliged to depend upon traveling performers, who, from time to time, engaged the Town Hall. Some time had elapsed since there had been any such entertainment, and Prof. Harrington was the more likely to be well patronized. Ben, who had the love of amusement common to boys of his age, had been regretting the necessity of remaining in the store till nine o'clock, and therefore losing his share of amusement when, as we have seen, an opportunity suddenly offered.

"I am glad I met the tramp, after all," he said to himself. "He has brought me luck."

Element Focus: Setting

Why is the setting important to the story?

Excerpt from

The Store Boy

by Horatio Alger Jr.

Ben Barclay, after taking leave of the tramp, lost no time in driving to the grocery store where he was employed. It was a large country store, devoted not to groceries alone, but supplies of dry goods, boots and shoes, and the leading articles required in the community. There were two other clerks besides Ben, one the son, another the nephew, of Simon Crawford, the proprietor.

"Did you collect any money, Ben?" asked Simon, who chanced to be standing at the door when our hero drove up.

"Yes, sir; I collected twenty-five dollars, but came near losing it on the way home."

"How was that? I hope you were not careless."

"No, except in taking a stranger as a passenger, and when we got to that piece of woods a mile back, he asked me for all the money I had."

"A highwayman, and so near Pentonville!" exclaimed Simon Crawford. "What was he like?"

"A regular tramp."

"Yet you say you have the money, so how did you manage to keep it from him?"

Ben detailed the stratagem of which he made use.

"You did well," said the storekeeper approvingly. "I must give you a dollar for the one you sacrificed."

"But sir, it was bad money, so I couldn't have passed it."

"That does not matter because you are entitled to some reward for the courage and quick wit you displayed. Here is a dollar, and, let me see, there is an entertainment at the Town Hall this evening, isn't there?"

"Yes, sir, Prof. Harrington, the magician, gives an entertainment," said Ben eagerly.

"At what time does it commence?"

"At eight o'clock."

"You may leave the store at half-past seven, and that will give you enough time to get there."

"Thank you, sir. I wanted to go to the entertainment, but did not like to ask for the evening off."

"You have earned it, and here is the dollar," and Mr. Crawford handed the money to his young clerk, who received it gratefully.

A magical entertainment may be a very common affair to my young readers in the city, but in a country village, it is an event. Pentonville was too small to have any regular place of amusement, and its citizens were obliged to depend upon traveling performers, who, from time to time, engaged the Town Hall. Some time had elapsed since there had been any such entertainment, and so Prof. Harrington was the more likely to be well patronized. Ben, who had the love of amusement common to boys of his age, had been regretting the necessity of remaining in the store till nine o'clock, and therefore losing his chance at amusement when, as we have seen, an opportunity suddenly offered.

"I am glad I met the tramp, after all," he said to himself. "He has brought me luck."

Element Focus: Setting

What setting would make the story
more exciting? Explain.

#50986—Leveled Texts for Classic Fiction: Historical Fiction
© Shell Education

The Rover Boys at School

by Edward Stratemeyer

They went into the station. They procured tickets. The time for the train had been changed. It would not be along for nearly half an hour.

"Good! Wait till I get back," said Tom.

He had noticed Ricks, the station master. Ricks was gathering some waste paper. He was looking around the depot. He felt tolerably certain that the old fellow was about to build a bonfire. He walked over to one of the stores. He entered. He asked the proprietor if he had any large firecrackers on hand.

"Just two," said the storekeeper. He brought them forth. Each was six inches long. They were thick in proportion.

"How much?" asked the boy.

"They are the last I have. I will let you have them for fifteen cents each."

"I will give you a quarter for the two."

"Very well. Here you are," said the storekeeper. The transfer was made on the spot. Tom slipped the firecrackers into his coat pocket. He sauntered up to old Ricks. Sam and Dick looked on. They were sure that something was in the wind.

"Ricks, that is pretty bad news from Middletown, isn't it?" he observed.

"Bad news? What do you mean?" demanded the station master. He had just lit a fire. He threw more waste paper on it.

"About that dynamite. It was stolen by train wreckers. They think some of the explosives was brought up here."

"Didn't hear of it."

"Dynamite is pretty bad stuff to have around. So I have heard."

"Awful! Awful! I never want to see any of it," answered Ricks. He made a decided shake of his head.

"It may go off. It is apt to blow everything to splinters," went on Dick.

"That is so. I don't want any of it," said the old man. He began to gather up more waste paper. He needed it for his fire. Tom watched for his chance. He threw one of the firecrackers into the blaze. Then he rejoined his brothers.

Ricks again approached the blaze. He had a handful of paper. He was standing almost over the fire. The firecracker went off. It made a tremendous sound. It scattered the light-blazing paper in all directions.

"Help! I am killed!" yelled old Ricks. He fell upon his back. "Get me away from here! There is dynamite in this fire!" He rolled over. He leapt to his feet. He ran off like a madman.

"Don't be alarmed. It was only a firecracker," called out Tom. He yelled loud enough for all standing around to hear. Then he ran for the train. It had just arrived. Soon he and his brothers were on board. They were off. They left poor Ricks behind. He was to be heartily laughed at by those who had observed the old man's sudden terror. It was many a day before the cranky station master heard the last of the dynamite story.

The boys were to ride from Oak Run to Ithaca. There they would take a small steamer. It ran from that city to the head of the lake. They were to stop at Cedarville. This was the nearest village to Putnam Hall. At Cedarville, one of the Hall conveyances was to meet them. It would transfer both them and their baggage to the institution.

Element Focus: Setting

What are the different settings
described in this passage?

#50986—*Leveled Texts for Classic Fiction: Historical Fiction*   © *Shell Education*

Excerpt from

The Rover Boys at School

by Edward Stratemeyer

They went into the station and procured tickets. They found the time for the train had been changed. It would not be along for nearly half an hour.

"Good! Just wait till I get back," said Tom.

He had noticed Ricks, the station master, gathering up some waste paper around the depot. He felt tolerably certain the old fellow was about to build a bonfire with it. Walking over to one of the stores, Tom entered. He asked the proprietor if he had any large firecrackers on hand.

"Just two, sir," said the storekeeper. He brought them forth. Each was six inches long and thick in proportion.

"How much?" asked the boy.

"They are the last I have. I'll let you have them for fifteen cents each."

"I'll give you a quarter for the two."

"Very well. Here you are," and the transfer was made on the spot. Tom slipped the firecrackers into his coat pocket. He sauntered up to old Ricks. Sam and Dick looked on. They were sure that something was in the wind.

"Ricks, that is pretty bad news from Middletown, isn't it?" he observed.

"Bad news? What do you mean?" demanded the station master. He threw some more waste paper on the fire that he had just lit.

"About that dynamite being stolen by train wreckers. They think some of the explosive was brought up here."

"Didn't hear of it."

"Dynamite is pretty bad stuff to have around. So I've heard."

"Awful! Awful! I never want to see any of it," answered Ricks, with a decided shake of his head.

"If it goes off, it's apt to blow everything to splinters," went on Dick.

"That's so—I don't want any of it," and the old man began to gather up more waste paper for his fire. Watching for his chance, Tom threw one of the firecrackers into the blaze and then rejoined his brothers.

With a handful of paper, Ricks again approached the blaze. He was standing almost over the fire when the firecracker went off, making a tremendous sound and scattering the light-blazing paper in all directions.

"Help! I'm killed!" yelled old Ricks, as he fell upon his back. "Get me away from here! There's dynamite in this fire!" And he rolled over, leapt to his feet, and ran off like a madman.

"Don't be alarmed. It was only a firecracker," called out Tom. He yelled loud enough for all standing around to hear. Then he ran for the train that had just arrived. Soon he and his brothers were on board and off. They left poor Ricks behind to be heartily laughed at by those who had observed the old man's sudden terror. It was many a day before the cranky station master heard the last of the dynamite story.

The boys were to ride from Oak Run to Ithaca. There they would take a small steamer that ran from that city to the head of the lake. They were to stop at Cedarville, the nearest village to Putnam Hall. At Cedarville, one of the Hall conveyances was to meet them. It would transfer both them and their baggage to the institution.

Element Focus: Setting

What is a possible explanation for the author selecting this setting?

#50986—Leveled Texts for Classic Fiction: Historical Fiction   © Shell Education

The Rover Boys at School

by Edward Stratemeyer

They went into the station and procured tickets, and then found the time for the train had been changed, and it would not be along for nearly half an hour.

"Good! Just wait till I get back," said Tom.

He had noticed Ricks gathering up some waste paper around the depot, and felt tolerably certain the old fellow was about to build a bonfire of it. Walking over to one of the stores, he entered, and asked the proprietor if he had any large firecrackers on hand.

"Just two, sir," said the storekeeper, and brought them forth. Each was six inches long and thick in proportion.

"How much?" asked the boy.

"Seeing as they are the last I have, I'll let you have them for fifteen cents each."

"I'll give you a quarter for the two."

"Very well; here you are," and the transfer was made on the spot. Slipping the firecrackers into his coat pocket, Tom sauntered up to old Ricks, while Sam and Dick looked on, sure that something was in the wind.

"Ricks, that is pretty bad news from Middletown, isn't it?" he observed.

"Bad news? What do you mean?" demanded the station master, as he threw some more waste paper on the fire, which he had just lit.

"About that dynamite being stolen by train wreckers. They think some of the explosive was brought up here."

"Didn't hear of it."

"Dynamite is pretty bad stuff to have around, so I've heard."

"Awful! Awful! I never want to see any of it," answered Ricks, with a decided shake of his head.

"If it goes off it's apt to blow everything to splinters," went on Dick.

"That's so—I don't want any of it," and the old man began to gather up more waste paper for his fire. Watching his chance, Tom threw one of the firecrackers into the blaze and then rejoined his brothers.

With a handful of paper Ricks again approached the blaze. He was standing almost over it when the firecracker went off, making a tremendous report and scattering the light blazing paper in all directions.

"Help! I'm killed!" yelled old Ricks, as he fell upon his back. "Get me away from here! There's dynamite in this fire!" And he rolled over, leapt to his feet, and ran off like a madman.

"Don't be alarmed—it was only a firecracker," called out Tom, loud enough for all standing around to hear, and then he ran for the train, which had just come in. Soon he and his brothers were on board and off, leaving poor Ricks to be heartily laughed at by those who had observed his sudden terror. It was many a day before the cranky station master heard the last of his dynamite.

The boys were to ride from Oak Run to Ithaca, and there take a small steamer which ran from that city to the head of the lake, stopping at Cedarville, the nearest village to Putnam Hall. At Cedarville one of the Hall conveyances was to meet them, to transfer both them and their baggage to the institution.

Element Focus: Setting

Explain a reason why the characters
fit well in this setting.

#50986—*Leveled Texts for Classic Fiction: Historical Fiction*   © *Shell Education*

The Rover Boys at School

by Edward Stratemeyer

They went into the station, procured tickets, and then found that the time for the train had been changed. It would not be along for nearly half an hour.

"Good, just wait till I get back," said Tom.

He had noticed Ricks, the station master, gathering up some waste paper around the depot, and felt tolerably certain the old fellow was about to build a bonfire with it. Walking over to one of the stores, Tom entered, and asked the proprietor if he had any large firecrackers on hand.

"Just two, sir," said the storekeeper, and brought them forth. He showed that each was six inches long and thick in proportion.

"How much?" asked the boy.

"Seeing as they are the last I have, I'll let you have them for fifteen cents each."

"I'll give you a quarter for the two."

"Very well, here you are," and the transfer was made on the spot. Then, slipping the firecrackers into his coat pocket, Tom sauntered up to old Ricks while Sam and Dick looked on, sure that something was in the wind.

"Ricks, that is pretty bad news from Middletown, isn't it?" he observed.

"Bad news, what do you mean?" demanded the station master, as he threw some more waste paper on the fire that he had just lit.

"About that dynamite being stolen by train wreckers. They think some of the explosive was brought up here."

"Didn't hear of it."

"Dynamite is pretty bad stuff to have around, so I've heard."

"Awful, awful, and I never want to see any of it," answered Ricks, with a decided shake of his head.

"If it goes off, it's apt to blow everything to splinters," went on Dick.

"That's so, and I don't want any of it," and the old man began to gather up more waste paper for his fire. Watching for his chance, Tom threw one of the firecrackers into the blaze and then rejoined his brothers.

With a handful of paper Ricks again approached the blaze and was standing almost over the fire when the firecracker went off. It made a tremendous sound and scattered the light-blazing paper in all directions.

"Help, I'm killed!" yelled old Ricks, as he fell upon his back. "Get me away from here, there's dynamite in this fire!" And he rolled over, leapt to his feet, and ran off like a madman.

"Don't be alarmed—it was only a firecracker," called out Tom, loud enough for all standing around to hear, and then he ran for the train, that had just arrived. Soon he and his brothers were on board and off, leaving behind poor Ricks to be heartily laughed at by those who had observed the old man's sudden terror. It was many a day before the cranky station master heard the last of the dynamite story.

The boys were to ride from Oak Run to Ithaca, and there take a small steamer that ran from that city to the head of the lake and stopped at Cedarville, the nearest village to Putnam Hall. At Cedarville, one of the Hall conveyances was to meet them to transfer both them and their baggage to the institution.

Element Focus: Setting

Following the correct sequence, describe where Tom and his brothers will travel on their journey.

#50986—Leveled Texts for Classic Fiction: Historical Fiction   © Shell Education

Excerpt from

The Prince and the Pauper

by Mark Twain

Poor little Tom was in his rags. He was moving slowly past the sentinels. He moved with a fast-beating heart. He felt a rising hope. He saw a spectacle. It almost made him shout for joy. Within was a comely boy. The boy was tanned and brown by playing sturdy outdoor sports and exercises. His clothing was all of lovely silks and satins. It was shining with jewels. He had a little jeweled sword and dagger. He had dainty buskins on his feet. They had red heels. He wore a jaunty crimson cap. It had drooping plumes fastened with a great sparkling gem. Several gorgeous gentlemen stood near. They were his servants. He was a prince! A real prince. Tom knew it without the shadow of a question. The prayer of the pauper boy's heart was answered at last.

Tom's breath came quick. It was cut short with excitement. His eyes grew big. He felt wonder and delight. He had one desire. He wanted to get close to the prince. He wanted to have a good, devouring look at him. Soon Tom had his face against the gate-bars. The next instant, one of the soldiers snatched him rudely away. He sent him spinning among the gaping crowd. The soldier said, "Mind thy manners, thou young beggar!"

The crowd jeered. They laughed. The young prince sprang to the gate. His face was flushed. His eyes were flashing with indignation. He cried out, "How dar'st thou use a poor lad like that? How dar'st thou use the King, my father's, meanest subject so? Open the gates. Let him in!"

You should have seen that fickle crowd. They snatched off their hats then. You should have heard them cheer. They shouted, "Long live the Prince of Wales!"

The soldiers presented arms with their halberds. They opened the gates. The little Prince of Poverty passed in. He was in his fluttering rags. He went to join hands with the Prince of Limitless Plenty.

Edward Tudor said, "Thou lookest tired and hungry. Thou'st been treated ill. Come with me."

Half a dozen attendants sprang forward to. To do I don't know what. Interfere, no doubt. They were waved aside with a right royal gesture. They stopped stock still where they were. They were like so many statues. Edward took Tom to a rich apartment in the palace. He called it his cabinet. By his command, a repast was brought. Tom had never encountered such a meal before except in books. The prince had both princely delicacy and breeding. He sent away his servants. He hoped his humble guest might not be embarrassed by their snobbish presence. Then the Prince sat near Tom. He asked questions while Tom ate.

"What is thy name, lad?"

"Tom Canty, an' it please thee, sir."

"'Tis an odd one. Where dost live?"

"In the city, please thee, sir. Offal Court, out of Pudding Lane."

"Offal Court! Truly 'tis another odd one. Hast parents?"

"Parents have I. A grand-dam likewise. Also twin sisters. Nan and Bet."

Element Focus: Character

Predict what the Prince will do next. Explain.

Excerpt from

The Prince and the Pauper

by Mark Twain

Poor little Tom, in his rags, approached. He was moving slowly and timidly past the sentinels. He moved with a fast-beating heart and a rising hope. All at once, he caught sight through the golden fence bars of a spectacle. It almost made him shout for joy. Within was a comely boy, tanned and brown by playing sturdy outdoor sports and exercises. His clothing was all of lovely silks and satins. It was shining with jewels. At his hip was a little jeweled sword and dagger. He had dainty buskins with red heels on his feet. On his head he wore a jaunty crimson cap. It had drooping plumes fastened with a great sparkling gem. Several gorgeous gentlemen stood near. They were his servants, without a doubt. Oh! He was a prince. A prince, a living prince, a real prince. Tom knew it without the shadow of a question. The prayer of the pauper boy's heart was answered at last.

Tom's breath came quick and short with excitement. His eyes grew big with wonder and delight. Everything gave way in his mind instantly to one desire. He wanted to get close to the prince. He wanted to have a good, devouring look at him. Before Tom knew what he was about, he had his face against the gate-bars. The next instant, one of the soldiers snatched him rudely away. He sent him spinning among the gaping crowd of country gawks and London idlers. The soldier said, "Mind thy manners, thou young beggar!"

The crowd jeered and laughed. The young prince sprang to the gate. His face was flushed, and his eyes were flashing with indignation. He cried out, "How dar'st thou use a poor lad like that? How dar'st thou use the King, my father's, meanest subject so? Open the gates, and let him in!"

You should have seen that fickle crowd snatch off their hats then. You should have heard them cheer, and shout, "Long live the Prince of Wales!"

The soldiers presented arms with their halberds. They opened the gates, and presented again as the little Prince of Poverty passed by, in his fluttering rags to join hands with the Prince of Limitless Plenty.

Edward Tudor said, "Thou lookest tired and hungry: thou'st been treated ill. Come with me."

Half a dozen attendants sprang forward to do—I don't know what; interfere, no doubt. But they were waved aside with a right royal gesture. They stopped stock still where they were like so many statues. Edward took Tom to a rich apartment in the palace. He called it his cabinet. By his command, a repast was brought such as Tom had never encountered before except in books. The prince, with princely delicacy and breeding, sent away the servants, so that his humble guest might not be embarrassed by their snobbish presence. Then the Prince sat near Tom. He asked questions while Tom ate.

"What is thy name, lad?"

"Tom Canty, an' it please thee, sir."

"'Tis an odd one. Where dost live?"

"In the city, please thee, sir. Offal Court, out of Pudding Lane."

"Offal Court! Truly 'tis another odd one. Hast parents?"

"Parents have I, sir. A grand-dam likewise that is but indifferently precious to me, God forgive me if it be offence to say it. Also twin sisters, Nan and Bet."

Element Focus: Character

For what reasons do you like or dislike Tom?

The Prince and the Pauper

by Mark Twain

Poor little Tom, in his rags, approached, and was moving slowly and timidly past the sentinels, with a beating heart and a rising hope, when all at once he caught sight through the golden bars of a spectacle that almost made him shout for joy. Within was a comely boy, tanned and brown with sturdy outdoor sports and exercises, whose clothing was all of lovely silks and satins, shining with jewels; at his hip a little jeweled sword and dagger; dainty buskins on his feet, with red heels; and on his head a jaunty crimson cap, with drooping plumes fastened with a great sparkling gem. Several gorgeous gentlemen stood near—his servants, without a doubt. Oh! He was a prince—a prince, a living prince, a real prince—without the shadow of a question; and the prayer of the pauper-boy's heart was answered at last.

Tom's breath came quick and short with excitement, and his eyes grew big with wonder and delight. Everything gave way in his mind instantly to one desire: that was to get close to the prince, and have a good, devouring look at him. Before he knew what he was about, he had his face against the gate-bars. The next instant one of the soldiers snatched him rudely away, and sent him spinning among the gaping crowd of country gawks and London idlers. The soldier said,—"Mind thy manners, thou young beggar!"

The crowd jeered and laughed; but the young prince sprang to the gate with his face flushed, and his eyes flashing with indignation, and cried out,—"How dar'st thou use a poor lad like that? How dar'st thou use the King my father's meanest subject so? Open the gates, and let him in!"

You should have seen that fickle crowd snatch off their hats then. You should have heard them cheer, and shout, "Long live the Prince of Wales!"

The soldiers presented arms with their halberds, opened the gates, and presented again as the little Prince of Poverty passed in, in his fluttering rags, to join hands with the Prince of Limitless Plenty.

Edward Tudor said—"Thou lookest tired and hungry: thou'st been treated ill. Come with me."

Half a dozen attendants sprang forward to—I don't know what; interfere, no doubt. But they were waved aside with a right royal gesture, and they stopped stock still where they were, like so many statues. Edward took Tom to a rich apartment in the palace, which he called his cabinet. By his command a repast was brought such as Tom had never encountered before except in books. The prince, with princely delicacy and breeding, sent away the servants, so that his humble guest might not be embarrassed by their critical presence; then he sat near by, and asked questions while Tom ate.

"What is thy name, lad?"

"Tom Canty, an' it please thee, sir."

"'Tis an odd one. Where dost live?"

"In the city, please thee, sir. Offal Court, out of Pudding Lane."

"Offal Court! Truly 'tis another odd one. Hast parents?"

"Parents have I, sir, and a grand-dam likewise that is but indifferently precious to me, God forgive me if it be offence to say it—also twin sisters, Nan and Bet."

Element Focus: Character

How did the prince treat Tom when they began to speak to each other? Why do you think he treated him in such way?

The Prince and the Pauper

by Mark Twain

Poor little Tom, in his rags, approached, and was moving slowly and timidly past the sentinels, with a beating heart and a rising hope, when all at once he caught sight through the golden bars of a spectacle that almost made him shout for joy. Within was a comely boy, tanned and brown with sturdy outdoor sports and exercises, whose clothing was all of lovely silks and satins, shining with jewels; at his hip a little jeweled sword and dagger; dainty buskins on his feet, with red heels; and on his head a jaunty crimson cap, with drooping plumes fastened with a great sparkling gem. Several gorgeous gentlemen stood near—his servants, without a doubt. He was a prince—a prince, a living prince, a real prince—without the shadow of a question; and the prayer of the pauper-boy's heart was answered at last.

Tom's breath came quick and short with excitement, his eyes grew big with wonder and delight, and everything gave way in his mind instantly to one desire: that was to get close to the prince, and have a good, devouring look at him. Before he knew what he was about, he had his face against the gate-bars. The next instant one of the soldiers snatched him rudely away, and sent him spinning among the gaping crowd of country gawks and London idlers. The soldier said,—"Mind thy manners, thou young beggar!"

The crowd jeered and laughed; but the young prince sprang to the gate with his face flushed, and his eyes flashing with indignation, and cried out,— "How dar'st thou use a poor lad like that, and how dar'st thou use the King my father's meanest subject so? Open the gates, and let him in!"

You should have seen that fickle crowd snatch off their hats then, and you should have heard them cheer, and shout, "Long live the Prince of Wales!"

The soldiers presented arms with their halberds, opened the gates, and presented again as the little Prince of Poverty passed in, in his fluttering rags, to join hands with the Prince of Limitless Plenty.

Edward Tudor said, "Thou lookest tired and hungry: thou'st been treated ill. Come with me."

Half a dozen attendants sprang forward to—I don't know what; interfere, no doubt. But they were waved aside with a right royal gesture, and they stopped stock still where they were, like so many statues. Edward took Tom to a rich apartment in the palace, which he called his cabinet, and by his command a repast was brought such as Tom had never encountered before except in books. The prince, with princely delicacy and breeding, sent away the servants, so that his humble guest might not be embarrassed by their critical presence; then he sat near by, and asked questions while Tom ate.

"What is thy name, lad?"

"Tom Canty, an' it please thee, sir."

"'Tis an odd one, but where dost live?"

"In the city, please thee, sir, at Offal Court, out of Pudding Lane."

"Offal Court! Truly 'tis another odd one. Hast parents?"

"Parents have I, sir, and a grand-dam likewise that is but indifferently precious to me, God forgive me if it be offence to say it—also twin sisters, Nan and Bet."

Element Focus: Character

In what ways are Tom and the prince different, and in what ways are they the same?

A Little Princess

by Frances Hodgson Burnett

Miss Minchin entered the room. She was like her house. She was tall and dull. She was also respectable and ugly. She had large eyes. They were cold and fishy. She also had a large smile. It was cold and fishy, too. She saw Sara and Captain Crewe. Her smile spread itself into a very large smile. She had heard a lot about the young soldier. A lady had told him about the school. She heard he was a rich father. He might spend a lot of money on the school.

"It will be a privilege to have such a beautiful child, Captain Crewe," she said. She took Sara's hand. She stroked it. "Lady Meredith has told me of her cleverness. A clever child is a great treasure in an establishment like mine."

Sara stood quietly. Her eyes were fixed. They watched Miss Minchin's face. She was thinking something odd.

"Why does she say that? Am I a beautiful child?" she thought. "I am not beautiful at all. Colonel Grange's little girl is beautiful. Isobel has dimples. She has rosy cheeks. She has long hair. It is the color of gold. I have black hair. I have green eyes. I am a thin child. I am not fair in the least. I am one of the ugliest children I ever saw. Miss Minchin is telling a story."

Sara was mistaken thinking she was ugly. She was not in the least like Isobel Grange. Isobel had been the beauty of the regiment. But Sara had an odd charm. She was a slim and supple creature. She was rather tall for her age. She was attractive. She had an intense little face. Her hair was heavy. It was quite black. It curled at the tips only. Her eyes were greenish gray. They were big, wonderful eyes. She had long, black lashes. Sara herself did not like the color of her eyes. Many other people did. Still, Sara was very firm in her belief. She thought she was an ugly little girl. She did not like Miss Minchin's flattery.

"I would be telling a story if I said Miss Minchin was beautiful," she thought. "I should know I was telling a story. I believe I am as ugly as she is. Why did she say I am pretty?"

Later Sara learned why Miss Minchin had said it. She discovered something. Miss Minchin said the same thing to each papa and mamma. Every parent heard the same words each time. When parents brought a child to Miss Minchin's school, Sara heard them.

Sara stood near her father. She listened. He talked to Miss Minchin. She had been brought to the school because of Lady Meredith. Lady Meredith's two girls had gone here. Captain Crewe respected Lady Meredith's experience. Sara was to be "a parlor-boarder." She would have greater privileges than parlor-boarders usually did. She was to have a pretty bedroom. She would also get a sitting-room of her own. She was to have a pony and a carriage. She would also have a maid. This maid would replace the ayah who had been her nurse in India.

"I am not worried about her education," Captain Crewe said. He had a gay laugh. He held Sara's hand. He patted it. "The hard part is keeping her from learning too fast and too much. She always has her nose in books. She does not read them. She gobbles them up. It is as if she were a little wolf instead of a little girl. She is always starving for new books to gobble. She wants grown-up books. She likes big and fat ones. She wants French and German. She wants English. She enjoys history. She likes biography. She enjoys poets. All sorts of things. Drag her away from her books. Do this when she reads too much. Make her ride her pony in the Row. Or go out and buy a new doll. She ought to play more with dolls."

Element Focus: Character

What are three things we learn about the character of Sara by reading this passage?

Excerpt from

A Little Princess

by Frances Hodgson Burnett

Miss Minchin entered the room. She was very much like her house. She was tall and dull. She was also respectable and ugly. She had large, cold, fishy eyes. She also had a large, cold, fishy smile. It spread itself into a very large smile when she saw Sara and Captain Crewe. She had heard many things about the young soldier from the lady who had recommended Miss Minchin's school to him. She had heard that he was a rich father. It was said that he would spend a great deal of money on his little daughter.

"It will be a great privilege to have charge of such a beautiful child, Captain Crewe," she said. She took Sara's hand. She stroked it. "Lady Meredith has told me of her cleverness. A clever child is a great treasure in an establishment like mine."

Sara stood quietly. Her eyes were fixed upon Miss Minchin's face. Sara thought something odd.

"Why does she say I am a beautiful child?" she thought. "I am not beautiful at all. Colonel Grange's little girl, Isobel, is beautiful. She has dimples and rose-colored cheeks. She has long hair the color of gold. I have black hair. I have green eyes. I am a thin child and not fair in the least. I am one of the ugliest children I ever saw. Miss Minchin is telling a story."

Sara was mistaken in thinking she was an ugly child. She was not in the least like Isobel Grange. Isobel had been the beauty of the regiment. But Sara had an odd charm of her own. She was a slim, supple creature. She was rather tall for her age. She had an intense, attractive little face. Her hair was heavy and quite black and only curled at the tips. Her eyes were greenish gray, it is true, but they were big, wonderful eyes with long, black lashes. Though she herself did not like the color of them, many other people did. Still Sara was very firm in her belief that she was an ugly little girl. She was not at all pleased by Miss Minchin's flattery.

"I should be telling a story if I said Miss Minchin was beautiful," she thought. "I should know I was telling a story. I believe I am as ugly as she is. Why did she say I am pretty?"

After Sara knew Miss Minchin longer, she learned why Miss Minchin had said it. Sara discovered something. Miss Minchin said the same thing to each papa and mamma who brought a child to her school.

Sara stood near her father. She listened while he and Miss Minchin talked. She had been brought to the school because Lady Meredith's two little girls had been educated here. Captain Crewe respected Lady Meredith's experience. Sara was to be what was known as "a parlor-boarder." She was to enjoy even greater privileges than parlor-boarders usually did. She was to have a pretty bedroom and sitting-room of her own. She was to have a pony and a carriage. She was also to have a maid to take the place of the ayah who had been her nurse in India.

"I am not in the least anxious about her education," Captain Crewe said. He had a gay laugh. He held Sara's hand and patted it. "The difficulty will be to keep her from learning too fast and too much. She is always sitting with her little nose burrowing into books. She doesn't read them, Miss Minchin. She gobbles them up. It is as if she were a little wolf instead of a little girl. She is always starving for new books to gobble. She wants grown-up books—great, big, fat ones. She wants French and German as well as English—history and biography and poetry. All sorts of things. Drag her away from her books when she reads too much. Make her ride her pony in the Row. Or go out and buy a new doll. She ought to play more with dolls."

Element Focus: Character

What words would you use to describe the character of Miss Minchin?

A Little Princess

by Frances Hodgson Burnett

It was just then that Miss Minchin entered the room. She was very like her house, Sara thought: tall and dull, respectable and ugly. She had large, cold, fishy eyes and a large, cold, fishy smile. When Miss Minchin saw Sara and Captain Crewe, her smile spread itself into a very large smile. Miss Minchin had heard a great many desirable things about the young soldier from the lady who had suggested her school to him. Among other things, Miss Minchin had heard that the captain was a rich father who was willing to spend a great deal of money on his little daughter.

"It will be a great joy to have charge of such a beautiful and promising child, Captain Crewe," she said, taking Sara's hand and stroking it. "Lady Meredith has told me of her rare cleverness. A clever child is a great prize in an establishment like mine."

Sara stood quietly, with her eyes fixed upon Miss Minchin's face. She was thinking something odd, as usual.

"Why does she say I am a pretty child?" she thought. "I am not pretty at all. Colonel Grange's little girl, Isobel, is pretty. She has dimples and rose-colored cheeks, and long hair the color of gold. I have black hair and green eyes. Besides, I am a thin child and not fair in the least. I am one of the ugliest children. Miss Minchin is beginning by telling a story."

Sara was wrong, however, in thinking she was an ugly child. She was not in the least like Isobel Grange, who had been the beauty of the regiment, but Sara had an odd charm of her own. She was a slim, limber creature, rather tall for her age, and she had an intense, cute little face. Her hair was heavy and quite black and only curled at the tips. Her eyes were greenish gray, it is true, but they were big, wonderful eyes with long, black lashes. Though she herself did not like the color of them, many other people did. She was not at all pleased by Miss Minchin's flattery.

"I should be telling a story if I said she was pretty," Sara thought; "and I should know I was telling a story. I believe I am as ugly as she is—in my way. Why did she say I am pretty?"

After Sara had known Miss Minchin longer, she learned why the woman had said it. She learned that Miss Minchin said the same thing to each papa and mamma who brought a child to her school.

Sara stood near her father and listened while he and Miss Minchin talked. She had been brought to the seminary because Lady Meredith's two little girls had been educated here. Captain Crewe had great respect for Lady Meredith's experience. Sara was to be what was known as "a parlor-boarder," and she was to enjoy even greater joys than parlor-boarders usually did. She was to have a pretty bedroom and a sitting-room of her own. She was to have a pony and a carriage, and a maid to take the place of the ayah who had been her nurse in India.

"I am not in the least worried about her education," Captain Crewe said, with his gay laugh, as he held Sara's hand and patted it. "The difficulty will be to keep her from learning too fast and too much. She is always sitting with her little nose burrowing into books. She does not read them, Miss Minchin. She gobbles them up as if she were a little wolf instead of a little girl. She is always starving for new books to gobble, and she wants grown-up books—great, big, fat ones—French and German as well as English—history and biography and poetry, and all sorts of things. Drag her away from her books when she reads too much. Make her ride her pony in the Row or go out and buy a new doll. She must play more with dolls."

Element Focus: Character

Why is Sara not flattered by Miss Minchin's kind words about her?

#50986—*Leveled Texts for Classic Fiction: Historical Fiction*   © *Shell Education*

A Little Princess

by Frances Hodgson Burnett

It was just then that Miss Minchin entered the room. She was very like her house, Sara felt: tall and dull, and respectable and ugly. She had large, cold, fishy eyes, and a large, cold, fishy smile. It spread itself into a very large smile when she saw Sara and Captain Crewe. She had heard a great many desirable things of the young soldier from the lady who had recommended her school to him. Among other things, she had heard that he was a rich father who was willing to spend a great deal of money on his little daughter.

"It will be a great privilege to have charge of such a beautiful and promising child, Captain Crewe," she said, taking Sara's hand and stroking it. "Lady Meredith has told me of her unusual cleverness. A clever child is a great treasure in an establishment like mine."

Sara stood quietly, with her eyes fixed upon Miss Minchin's face. She was thinking something odd, as usual.

"Why does she say I am a beautiful child?" she was thinking. "I am not beautiful at all. Colonel Grange's little girl, Isobel, is beautiful. She has dimples and rose-colored cheeks, and long hair the color of gold. I have black hair and green eyes; besides which, I am a thin child and not fair in the least. I am one of the ugliest children I ever saw. She is beginning by telling a story."

She was mistaken, however, in thinking she was an ugly child. She was not in the least like Isobel Grange, who had been the beauty of the regiment, but she had an odd charm of her own. She was a slim, supple creature, rather tall for her age, and had an intense, attractive little face. Her hair was heavy and quite black and only curled at the tips; her eyes were greenish gray, it is true, but they were big, wonderful eyes with long, black lashes, and though she herself did not like the color of them, many other people did. Still she was very firm in her belief that she was an ugly little girl, and she was not at all elated by Miss Minchin's flattery.

"I should be telling a story if I said she was beautiful," she thought; "and I should know I was telling a story. I believe I am as ugly as she is—in my way. What did she say that for?"

After she had known Miss Minchin longer she learned why she had said it. She discovered that she said the same thing to each papa and mamma who brought a child to her school.

Sara stood near her father and listened while he and Miss Minchin talked. She had been brought to the seminary because Lady Meredith's two little girls had been educated there, and Captain Crewe had a great respect for Lady Meredith's experience. Sara was to be what was known as "a parlor-boarder," and she was to enjoy even greater privileges than parlor-boarders usually did. She was to have a pretty bedroom and sitting-room of her own; she was to have a pony and a carriage, and a maid to take the place of the ayah who had been her nurse in India.

"I am not in the least anxious about her education," Captain Crewe said, with his gay laugh, as he held Sara's hand and patted it. "The difficulty will be to keep her from learning too fast and too much. She is always sitting with her little nose burrowing into books. She doesn't read them, Miss Minchin; she gobbles them up as if she were a little wolf instead of a little girl. She is always starving for new books to gobble, and she wants grown-up books—great, big, fat ones—French and German as well as English—history and biography and poets, and all sorts of things. Drag her away from her books when she reads too much. Make her ride her pony in the Row or go out and buy a new doll. She ought to play more with dolls."

Element Focus: Character

What does Sara think of Miss Minchin?
How do you know?

Rainbow Valley

by Lucy Maud Montgomery

A girl was curled up. She was in a little nest in the hay. She looked as if she had just wakened. She stood up. She stood rather shakily. Bright sunlight streamed through the cobwebbed window behind her. They saw her thin, sunburned face. It was very pale under its tan. She had two braids. They were made from lank, thick, blond-coloured hair. She also had very odd eyes. They were "white eyes," the manse children thought. She stared at them half defiantly, half piteously. Here eyes were really so pale a blue that they did seem almost white. The pale colour contrasted with the narrow black ring that circled the iris. She was barefooted and bareheaded. She was clad in a ragged and old plaid dress. It was much too short for her. It was also too tight. She might have been almost any age. Yet her height seemed to suggest she was around twelve years old.

"Who are you?" asked Jerry.

The girl looked about her. It was as if she was seeking a way of escape. Then she seemed to give in. She felt a little shiver of despair.

"I am Mary Vance," she said.

"Where did you come from?" pursued Jerry.

Mary did not reply. Suddenly she sat, or fell. She went down on the hay. She began to cry. Faith flung herself down beside her. She put her arm around the girl. Mary had thin, shaking shoulders.

"You stop bothering her," Faith commanded Jerry. Then she hugged the waif. "Don't cry, dear. Tell us what is the matter. We ARE friends."

"I am so hungry," wailed Mary. "I have not had a thing to eat since Thursday morning. I only had a little water from the brook out there."

The manse children gazed at each other in horror. Faith sprang up.

"You come right up to the manse. Get something to eat before you say another word."

Mary shrank.

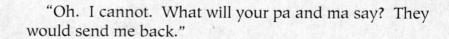

"Oh. I cannot. What will your pa and ma say? They would send me back."

"We have no mother. Father will not bother about you. Neither will Aunt Martha. Come, I say." Faith stamped her foot impatiently. Was this queer girl going to insist on starving to death when she was almost at their very door?

Mary yielded. She was so weak. She could hardly climb down the ladder. Somehow they got her down. They went over the field. They walked into the manse kitchen. Aunt Martha was muddling through her Saturday cooking. She took no notice of her. Faith and Una flew to the pantry. They ransacked it for such eatables as it contained. They found some "ditto" bread, butter, milk, and a doubtful pie. Mary Vance attacked the food ravenously and uncritically. The manse children stood around. They watched her. Jerry noticed that she had a pretty mouth. She had very nice, even, white teeth. Faith decided, with secret horror, that Mary was not wearing one stitch of clothing except for that ragged, faded dress. Una was full of pure pity. Carl was full of amused wonder. All of them were full of curiosity.

Element Focus: Character

In what way does Mary Vance show her thoughts through her actions?

#50986—*Leveled Texts for Classic Fiction: Historical Fiction*　　　© Shell Education

Excerpt from

Rainbow Valley

by Lucy Maud Montgomery

In a little nest in the hay, a girl was curled up. She looked as if she had just wakened from sleep. When she saw the children, she stood up rather shakily. Bright sunlight streamed through the cobwebbed window behind her. They saw that her thin, sunburned face was very pale under its tan. She had two braids of lank, thick, blond-coloured hair and very odd eyes—"white eyes," the manse children thought. She stared at them half defiantly, half piteously. Her eyes were really so pale a blue that they did seem almost white, especially when contrasted with the narrow black ring that circled the iris. She was barefooted and bareheaded. She was clad in a faded, ragged, old plaid dress, much too short and tight for her. As for years, she might have been almost any age, judging from her wizened little face. Yet her height seemed to suggest she was somewhere in the neighbourhood of twelve.

"Who are you?" asked Jerry.

The girl looked about her as if seeking a way of escape. Then she seemed to give in with a little shiver of despair.

"I'm Mary Vance," she said.

"Where'd you come from?" pursued Jerry.

Mary, instead of replying, suddenly sat, or fell, down on the hay. She began to cry. Instantly Faith flung herself down beside her. She put her arm around the girl's thin, shaking shoulders.

"You stop bothering her," Faith commanded Jerry. Then she hugged the waif. "Don't cry, dear. Just tell us what's the matter. We ARE friends."

"I am so hungry," wailed Mary. "I have not had a thing to eat since Thursday morning. I only had a little water from the brook out there."

The manse children gazed at each other in horror. Faith sprang up.

"You come right up to the manse. Get something to eat before you say another word."

Mary shrank.

"Oh. I can't. What will your pa and ma say? Besides, they would send me back."

"We have no mother. Father will not bother about you. Neither will Aunt Martha. Come, I say." Faith stamped her foot impatiently. Was this queer girl going to insist on starving to death almost at their very door?

Mary yielded. She was so weak that she could hardly climb down the ladder. Somehow they got her down and over the field and into the manse kitchen. Aunt Martha was muddling through her Saturday cooking. She took no notice of her. Faith and Una flew to the pantry. They ransacked it for such eatables as it contained. They found some "ditto" bread, butter, milk, and a doubtful pie. Mary Vance attacked the food ravenously and uncritically. The manse children stood around and watched her. Jerry noticed that she had a pretty mouth and very nice, even, white teeth. Faith decided, with secret horror, that Mary was not wearing one stitch except for that ragged, faded dress. Una was full of pure pity. Carl was full of amused wonder. All of them were full of curiosity.

Element Focus: Character

What makes the character of Mary Vance memorable?

Rainbow Valley

by Lucy Maud Montgomery

In a little nest in the hay a girl was curled up, looking as if she had just wakened from sleep. When she saw them she stood up, rather shakily, as it seemed, and in the bright sunlight that streamed through the cobwebbed window behind her, they saw that her thin, sunburned face was very pale under its tan. She had two braids of lank, thick, tow-coloured hair and very odd eyes—"white eyes," the manse children thought, as she stared at them half defiantly, half piteously. They were really of so pale a blue that they did seem almost white, especially when contrasted with the narrow black ring that circled the iris. She was barefooted and bareheaded, and was clad in a faded, ragged, old plaid dress, much too short and tight for her. As for years, she might have been almost any age, judging from her wizened little face, but her height seemed to be somewhere in the neighbourhood of twelve.

"Who are you?" asked Jerry.

The girl looked about her as if seeking a way of escape. Then she seemed to give in with a little shiver of despair.

"I'm Mary Vance," she said.

"Where'd you come from?" pursued Jerry.

Mary, instead of replying, suddenly sat, or fell, down on the hay and began to cry. Instantly Faith had flung herself down beside her and put her arm around the thin, shaking shoulders.

"You stop bothering her," she commanded Jerry. Then she hugged the waif. "Don't cry, dear. Just tell us what's the matter. WE'RE friends."

"I'm so—so—hungry," wailed Mary. "I—I hain't had a thing to eat since Thursday morning, 'cept a little water from the brook out there."

The manse children gazed at each other in horror. Faith sprang up.

"You come right up to the manse and get something to eat before you say another word."

Mary shrank.

"Oh—I can't. What will your pa and ma say? Besides, they'd send me back."

"We've no mother, and father won't bother about you. Neither will Aunt Martha. Come, I say." Faith stamped her foot impatiently. Was this queer girl going to insist on starving to death almost at their very door?

Mary yielded. She was so weak that she could hardly climb down the ladder, but somehow they got her down and over the field and into the manse kitchen. Aunt Martha, muddling through her Saturday cooking, took no notice of her. Faith and Una flew to the pantry and ransacked it for such eatables as it contained—some "ditto," bread, butter, milk and a doubtful pie. Mary Vance attacked the food ravenously and uncritically, while the manse children stood around and watched her. Jerry noticed that she had a pretty mouth and very nice, even, white teeth. Faith decided, with secret horror, that Mary had not one stitch on her except that ragged, faded dress. Una was full of pure pity, Carl of amused wonder, and all of them of curiosity.

Element Focus: Character

What are some ways you would improve Mary Vance's description?

#50986—Leveled Texts for Classic Fiction: Historical Fiction

Rainbow Valley

by Lucy Maud Montgomery

In a little nest in the hay a girl was curled up, looking as if she had just wakened from sleep. When she saw the children, she stood up rather shakily as it seemed, and in the bright sunlight that streamed through the cobwebbed window behind her, they saw that her thin, sunburned face was very pale under its tan. She had two braids of lank, thick, blond-coloured hair and very odd eyes—"white eyes," the manse children thought, as she stared at them half defiantly, half piteously. Her eyes were really so pale a blue that they did seem almost white, especially when contrasted with the narrow black ring that circled the iris. She was barefooted, bareheaded, and clad in a faded, ragged, old plaid dress, much too short and tight for her. As for years, she might have been almost any age, judging from her wizened little face, but her height seemed to suggest she was somewhere in the neighbourhood of twelve.

"Who are you?" asked Jerry.

The girl looked about her as if seeking a way of escape, and then she seemed to give in with a little shiver of despair.

"I'm Mary Vance," she said.

"Where'd you come from?" pursued Jerry.

Mary, instead of replying, suddenly sat, or fell, down on the hay and began to cry. Instantly Faith flung herself down beside her and put her arm around the girl's thin, shaking shoulders.

"You stop bothering her," Faith commanded Jerry, and then she hugged the waif. "Don't cry, dear, just tell us what's the matter. WE'RE friends."

"I'm so—so—hungry," wailed Mary. "I—I hain't had a thing to eat since Thursday morning, 'cept a little water from the brook out there."

The manse children gazed at each other in horror as Faith sprang up.

"You come right up to the manse and get something to eat before you say another word."

Mary shrank.

"Oh—I can't. What will your pa and ma say? Besides, they'd send me back."

"We've no mother, and father won't bother about you, and neither will Aunt Martha, so come, I say." Faith stamped her foot impatiently. Was this queer girl going to insist on starving to death almost at their very door?

Mary yielded, as she was so weak that she could hardly climb down the ladder, but somehow they got her down and over the field and into the manse kitchen. Aunt Martha, muddling through her Saturday cooking, took no notice of her, and Faith and Una flew to the pantry, ransacking it for such eatables as it contained— some "ditto" bread, butter, milk, and a doubtful pie. Mary Vance attacked the food ravenously and uncritically, while the manse children stood around and watched her. Jerry noticed that she had a pretty mouth and very nice, even, white teeth, while Faith decided, with secret horror, that Mary was wearing not one stitch except that ragged, faded dress. Una was full of pure pity, Carl of amused wonder, and all of them of curiosity.

Element Focus: Character

What are some things you learned about Mary Vance from reading this passage?

#50986—Leveled Texts for Classic Fiction: Historical Fiction   © Shell Education

Little Women

by Louisa May Alcott

To Jo's lively fancy, this fine house seemed a kind of enchanted palace. It was full of splendors and delights that no one enjoyed. She had long wanted to behold these hidden glories. She wanted to know the Laurence boy. He looked as though he would like to be known, if only he knew how to begin. Since the party, Jo had been more eager than ever. She had planned many ways of making friends with him. But she had not seen Laurie lately. Jo began to think he had gone away. One day, she spied a brown face at an upper window. It was looking wistfully down into their garden. Beth and Amy were snow-balling one another.

"That boy is suffering for lack of society and fun," she said to herself. "His grandpa does not know what is good for him. He keeps him shut up all alone. He needs a party of jolly boys to play with. He needs somebody young and lively. I want to go over and tell the old man so!"

The idea amused Jo. Jo liked to do daring things. She was always scandalizing Meg by her strange actions. The plan of "going over" was not forgotten. Soon a snowy afternoon came. Jo resolved to try what she could. She saw Mr. Laurence drive off. Then she sallied out to dig her way down to the hedge. She paused. She took a survey. All was quiet. The curtains were down at the lower windows. The servants were out of sight. Nothing human was visible but a curly black head. It was leaning on a thin hand. It was at the upper window.

"There he is," thought Jo, "Poor boy! All alone and sick on this dismal day. It is a shame! I will toss up a snowball. It will make him look out. Then I can say a kind word to him."

Up went a handful of soft snow. The head turned at once. The face lost its listless look in a minute. The big eyes brightened and the mouth began to smile. Jo nodded and laughed. She flourished her broom as she called out, "How do you do? Are you sick?"

Laurie opened the window, and croaked out as hoarsely as a raven, "Better, thank you. I have had a bad cold. I have been shut up a week."

"I am sorry. What do you amuse yourself with?"

"Nothing. It is dull as tombs up here."

"Don't you read?"

"Not much. They won't let me."

"Can't somebody read to you?"

"Grandpa does sometimes. But my books do not interest him. I hate to ask Brooke all the time."

"Have someone come and see you then."

"There isn't anyone I'd like to see. Boys make such a row. My head is weak."

"Isn't there some nice girl who'd read and amuse you? Girls are quiet and like to play nurse."

"Don't know any."

"You know us," began Jo. Then she laughed and stopped.

"So I do! Will you come, please?" cried Laurie.

"I am not quiet and nice. But I will come if Mother will let me. I will go ask her. Shut the window. Be a good boy. Wait till I come."

Element Focus: Character

Predict what Jo will do next. Explain.

Excerpt from

Little Women

by Louisa May Alcott

To Jo's lively fancy, this fine house seemed a kind of enchanted palace, full of splendors and delights which no one enjoyed. She had long wanted to behold these hidden glories, and to know the Laurence boy, who looked as if he would like to be known, if he only knew how to begin. Since the party, she had been more eager than ever, and had planned many ways of making friends with him, but he had not been seen lately, and Jo began to think he had gone away, when she one day spied a brown face at an upper window, looking wistfully down into their garden, where Beth and Amy were snow-balling one another.

"That boy is suffering for society and fun," she said to herself. "His grandpa does not know what's good for him, and keeps him shut up all alone. He needs a party of jolly boys to play with, or somebody young and lively. I've a great mind to go over and tell the old gentleman so!"

The idea amused Jo, who liked to do daring things and was always scandalizing Meg by her strange performances. The plan of 'going over' was not forgotten. And when the snowy afternoon came, Jo resolved to try what could be done. She saw Mr. Laurence drive off, and then sallied out to dig her way down to the hedge, where she paused and took a survey. All quiet, curtains down at the lower windows, servants out of sight, and nothing human visible but a curly black head leaning on a thin hand at the upper window.

"There he is," thought Jo, "Poor boy! All alone and sick this dismal day. It's a shame! I'll toss up a snowball and make him look out, and then say a kind word to him."

Up went a handful of soft snow, and the head turned at once, showing a face which lost its listless look in a minute, as the big eyes brightened and the mouth began to smile. Jo nodded and laughed, and flourished her broom as she called out..."How do you do? Are you sick?"

Laurie opened the window, and croaked out as hoarsely as a raven..."Better, thank you. I've had a bad cold, and been shut up a week."

"I'm sorry. What do you amuse yourself with?"

"Nothing. It's dull as tombs up here."

"Don't you read?"

"Not much. They won't let me."

"Can't somebody read to you?"

"Grandpa does sometimes, but my books don't interest him, and I hate to ask Brooke all the time."

"Have someone come and see you then."

"There isn't anyone I'd like to see. Boys make such a row, and my head is weak."

"Isn't there some nice girl who'd read and amuse you? Girls are quiet and like to play nurse."

"Don't know any."

"You know us," began Jo, then laughed and stopped.

"So I do! Will you come, please?" cried Laurie.

"I'm not quiet and nice, but I'll come, if Mother will let me. I'll go ask her. Shut the window, like a good boy, and wait till I come."

Element Focus: Character

Explain a reason for Jo's decision to talk to the boy.

Excerpt from

Little Women

by Louisa May Alcott

To Jo's lively fancy, this fine house seemed a kind of enchanted palace, full of splendors and delights that no one enjoyed. She had long wanted to behold these hidden glories and to know the Laurence boy, who looked as though he would like to be known if only he knew how to begin. Since the party, Jo had been more eager than ever, and had planned many ways of making friends with him. She had not seen Laurie lately and began to think he had gone away. Then one day she spied a brown face at an upper window, looking wistfully down into their garden where Beth and Amy were snow-balling one another.

"That boy is suffering for lack of society and fun," she said to herself. "His grandpa does not know what's good for him and keeps him shut up all alone, but he needs a party of jolly boys to play with or somebody young and lively. I've a great mind to go over and tell the old gentleman so!"

The idea amused Jo, who liked to do daring things and was always scandalizing Meg by her strange behavior. The plan of "going over" was not forgotten, and when a snowy afternoon came, Jo resolved to try what she could. She saw Mr. Laurence drive off, and then sallied out to dig her way down to the hedge, where she paused and took a survey of what she saw—all was quiet, curtains down at the lower windows, servants out of sight, and nothing human visible but a curly black head leaning on a thin hand at the upper window.

"There he is," thought Jo, "Poor boy who is all alone and sick on this dismal day. It's a shame! I'll toss up a snowball to make him look out and then say a kind word to him."

Up went a handful of soft snow, and the head turned at once, showing a face which lost its listless look in a minute, as the big eyes brightened and the mouth began to smile. Jo nodded and laughed, and flourished her broom as she called out, "How do you do, and are you sick?"

Laurie opened the window, and croaked out as hoarsely as a raven..."Better, thank you, but I've had a bad cold, and been shut up a week."

"I'm sorry, but what do you amuse yourself with?"

"Nothing, because it's dull as tombs up here."

"Don't you read?"

"Not much. They won't let me."

"Can't somebody read to you?"

"Grandpa does sometimes, but my books don't interest him, and I hate to ask Brooke all the time."

"Have someone come and see you then."

"There isn't anyone I'd like to see because boys make such a row, and my head is weak."

"Isn't there some nice girl who'd read and amuse you? Girls are quiet and like to play nurse."

"Don't know any."

"You know us," began Jo, then laughed and stopped.

"So I do! Will you come, please?" cried Laurie.

"I'm not quiet and nice, but I'll come, if Mother will let me. I'll go ask her. Shut the window like a good boy and wait till I come."

Element Focus: Character

Is Jo acting like a good friend in this passage? Why or why not?

#50986—Leveled Texts for Classic Fiction: Historical Fiction

Excerpt from

Little Women

by Louisa May Alcott

To Jo's lively fancy, this fine house seemed a kind of enchanted palace, full of splendors and delights that no one appreciated. She had long wanted to behold these hidden glories, and to know the Laurence boy, who looked as if he would like to be known, if only he knew how to introduce himself. Since the celebration, Jo had been more impatient than ever and had planned many ways of making friends with him. She had not seen Laurie recently and began to think he had gone away. Then one day she spied a brown face at an upper window, looking wistfully down into their garden where Beth and Amy were snow-balling one another.

"That boy is suffering for lack of society and fun," she said to herself. "His grandpa does not know what's good for him and keeps him shut up all alone, but he needs a party of jolly boys to play with or somebody young and lively. I've a great mind to go over and tell the old gentleman so!"

The idea amused Jo, who liked to do daring things and was always scandalizing Meg by her strange behavior. The plan of "going over" was not discarded, and when a snowy afternoon came, Jo resolved to try what she could. She saw Mr. Laurence drive off, and then sallied out to dig her way down to the hedge, where she paused and took a survey of what she observed—all was quiet, curtains down at the lower windows, servants out of sight, and nothing human detectable but a curly black head leaning on a thin hand at the upper window.

"There he is," thought Jo, "Poor boy who is all alone and sick on this dismal day. It's a shame! I'll toss up a snowball to make him look out and then say a kind word to him."

Up went a handful of soft snow, and the head turned at once, showing a face that lost its listless look in a minute, as the big eyes brightened and the mouth began to smile. Jo nodded and laughed, and flourished her broom as she called out, "How do you do, and are you sick?"

Laurie opened the window, and croaked out as hoarsely as a raven, "Better, thank you, but I've had a bad cold, and been shut up a week."

"I'm sorry, but what do you amuse yourself with?"

"Nothing, because it's tedious as tombs up here."

"Don't you read?"

"Not much. They won't let me."

"Can't somebody read to you?"

"Grandpa does sometimes, but my books don't interest him, and I hate to ask Brooke all the time."

"Have someone come and see you then."

"There isn't anyone I'd like to see because boys make such a row, and my head is weak."

"Isn't there some nice girl who'd read and amuse you? Girls are quiet and like to play nurse."

"Don't know any."

"You know us," began Jo, then laughed and stopped.

"So I do! Will you come, please?" cried Laurie.

"I'm not quiet and nice, but I'll come, if Mother will let me. I'll go ask her. Shut the window like a good boy, and wait till I come."

Element Focus: Character

Describe Jo's actions in this passage?

#50986—Leveled Texts for Classic Fiction: Historical Fiction
© Shell Education

Excerpt from

The Lords of the Wild

by Joseph A. Altsheler

"Do you feel sure that they will attack tonight?" he asked Willet. "Perhaps St. Luc will see the strength of our position. He may draw off. Or he may send to Montcalm for cannon. That doubtless would take a week."

The hunter shook his head.

"St. Luc will not go away," Willet said. "He will not send for cannon. It would take too long. He will not use his strength alone. He will depend also upon wile and stratagem. We must guard against that every minute. I think I will take my own men. We will go outside. We can be of more service there."

"I suppose you are right. Do not walk into danger. I depend a lot on you."

Willet climbed over the logs. Tayoga followed. So did Robert and Grosvenor.

"Red Coat buckled on a sword. I did not think he would go on a trail again," said Tayoga.

"One instance in which you did not read my mind right," rejoined the Englishman. "I know that swords do not belong on the trail. This is only a little blade. You fellows cannot leave me behind."

"I did read your mind right," said Tayoga. "I merely spoke of your sword to see what you would say. I knew you would come with us."

The tree stumps stretched far away. They went on for a distance of several hundred yards. The stumps were left after the forest had been cut away. The dark shadow of Black Rifle came forward.

"Nothing yet?" asked the hunter.

"Nothing so far. Three or four good men are with me among the stumps. Not a warrior has yet appeared. I suppose they know we will be on watch here. It is not worth taking so great a risk."

They advanced. They moved to the far edge of the stump region. They crouched there. The night was now quite dark. The moon was almost hidden. There were few stars. The forest was a solid black line before them.

"Why can't Tayoga use his ears?" said Grosvenor. "He will hear them a mile away."

"A little farther on and he will," replied Willet. "We do not dare to go deep into the forest."

They went a hundred yards more. The Onondaga put his ear to the ground. It was a long time before he announced anything.

"I hear footsteps fairly near to us," he said at last. "I think they are those of warriors. They should be more cautious. But they do not believe we are outside the line of log stumps. Yes, they are warriors. All warriors. There is no jingle of metal such as the French have on their coats or belts. They are trying to take a look at our position. They are about to pass now to our right. I also hear other steps. They are farther away. They are on our left. I think they are steps of those Frenchmen."

"Likely De Courcelles and Jumonville who want also to look us over," said Willet.

"There is another and larger force coming directly toward us," continued the Onondaga. "I think it includes both the French and the warriors. This may be the attack. Perhaps it would be better for us to fall back."

Element Focus: Plot

What suspenseful event is happening in this story?

#50986—Leveled Texts for Classic Fiction: Historical Fiction

The Lords of the Wild

by Joseph A. Altsheler

"Do you feel sure that they will attack tonight?" he asked Willet. "Perhaps St. Luc, seeing the strength of our position, will draw off or send to Montcalm for cannon, which doubtless would take a week."

The hunter shook his head.

"St. Luc will not go away," Willet said. "He will not send for cannon. It would take too long. He will not use his strength alone. He will depend also upon wile and stratagem, against which we must guard every minute. I think I will take my own men and go outside. We can be of more service there."

"I suppose you are right. Don't walk into danger. I depend a lot on you."

Willet climbed over the logs. Tayoga, Robert, and Grosvenor followed.

"Red Coat buckled on a sword, and I did not think he would go on a trail again," said Tayoga.

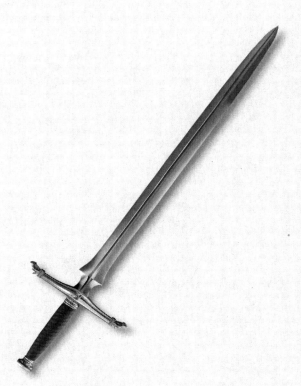

"One instance in which you did not read my mind right," rejoined the Englishman. "I know that swords don't belong on the trail. This is only a little blade. You fellows can't leave me behind."

"I did read your mind right," said Tayoga. "I merely spoke of your sword to see what you would say. I knew all the time that you would come with us."

The stumps stretched for a distance of several hundred yards. A little distance from the breastwork, the dark shadow of Black Rifle came forward to meet Willet and his men.

"Nothing yet?" asked the hunter.

"Nothing so far. Three or four good men are with me among the stumps. Not a warrior has yet appeared. I suppose they know we will be on watch here. It is not worth taking so great a risk."

They advanced to the far edge of the stump region and crouched there. The night was now quite dark. The moon was almost hidden, the stars but few. The forest was a solid black line before them.

"Why can't Tayoga use his ears?" said Grosvenor. "He will hear them even a mile away."

"A little farther on and he will," replied Willet, "but we, in our turn, don't dare to go deep into the forest."

A hundred yards more and Tayoga, the Onondaga, put his ear to the ground. It was a long time before he announced anything.

"I hear footsteps fairly near to us," he said at last, "and I think they are those of warriors. They would be more cautious, but they do not believe we are outside the line of logs. Yes, they are warriors, all warriors. There is no jingle of metal such as the French have on their coats or belts. They are trying to take a look at our position. They are about to pass now to our right. I also hear other steps, but farther away, on our left. I think they are the steps of those Frenchmen."

"Likely De Courcelles and Jumonville who want also to look us over," said Willet.

"There is another and larger force coming directly toward us," continued the Onondaga. "I think it includes both the French and the warriors. This may be the attack. Perhaps it would be better for us to fall back."

Element Focus: Plot

What are possible results that could occur in this scene?

The Lords of the Wild

by Joseph A. Altsheler

"Do you feel sure that they will attack tonight?" he asked Willet. "Perhaps St. Luc, seeing the strength of our position, will draw off or send to Montcalm for cannon, which doubtless would take a week."

The hunter shook his head.

"St. Luc will not go away," he said, "nor will he send for cannon, which would take too long. He will not use his strength alone, he will depend also upon wile and stratagem, against which we must guard every minute. I think I'll take my own men and go outside. We can be of more service there."

"I suppose you're right, but don't walk into danger. I depend a lot on you."

Willet climbed over the logs. Tayoga, Robert, and Grosvenor followed.

"Red Coat buckled on a sword, and I did not think he would go on a trail again," said Tayoga.

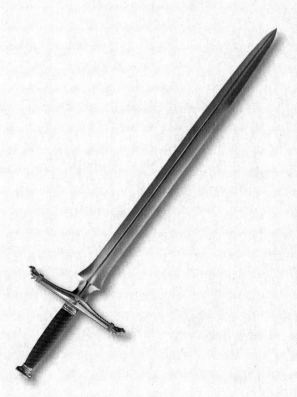

"One instance in which you didn't read my mind right," rejoined the Englishman. "I know that swords don't belong on the trail, but this is only a little blade, and you fellows can't leave me behind."

"I did read your mind right," said Tayoga, laughing softly. "I merely spoke of your sword to see what you would say. I knew all the time that you would come with us."

The stumps, where the forest had been cut away, stretched for a distance of several hundred yards up the slope, and, a little distance from the breastwork, the dark shadow of Black Rifle came forward to meet them.

"Nothing yet?" asked the hunter.

"Nothing so far. Three or four good men are with me among the stumps, but not a warrior has yet appeared. I suppose they know we'll be on watch here, and it's not worth while taking so great a risk."

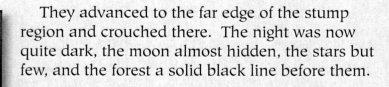

They advanced to the far edge of the stump region and crouched there. The night was now quite dark, the moon almost hidden, the stars but few, and the forest a solid black line before them.

"Why can't Tayoga use his ears?" said Grosvenor. "He'll hear them, though a mile away."

"A little farther on and he will," replied Willet, "but we, in our turn, don't dare to go deep into the forest."

A hundred yards more and the Onondaga put ear to earth, but it was a long time before he announced anything.

"I hear footsteps fairly near to us," he said at last, "and I think they are those of warriors. They would be more cautious, but they do not believe we are outside the line of logs. Yes, they are warriors, all warriors, there is no jingle of metal such as the French have on their coats or belts, and they are going to take a look at our position. They are about to pass now to our right. I also hear steps, but farther away, on our left, and I think they are those of Frenchmen."

"Likely De Courcelles and Jumonville wanting also to look us over," said Willet.

"There is another and larger force coming directly toward us," continued the Onondaga, "and I think it includes both French and warriors. This may be the attack and perhaps it would be better for us to fall back."

Element Focus: Plot

How does the action build in this story, from beginning to end?

Excerpt from

The Lords of the Wild

by Joseph A. Altsheler

"Do you feel sure that they will attack tonight?" he asked Willet. "Perhaps St. Luc, seeing the strength of our position, will draw off or send to Montcalm for cannon, which doubtless would take a week."

The hunter shook his head.

"St. Luc will not go away," Willet said, "nor will he send for cannon, which would take too long. He will not use his strength alone, but will depend also upon wile and stratagem, against which we must guard every minute. I think I'll take my own men and go outside since we can be of more service there."

"I suppose you're right, but don't walk into danger because I depend a lot on you."

Willet climbed over the logs as Tayoga, Robert, and Grosvenor followed.

"Red Coat buckled on a sword, and I did not think he would go on a trail again," said Tayoga.

"One instance in which you didn't read my mind right," rejoined the Englishman. "I know that swords don't belong on the trail, but this is only a little blade, and you fellows can't leave me behind."

"I did read your mind right," said Tayoga, "but I merely spoke of your sword. I knew all the time that you would come with us."

The stumps, where the forest had been cut away, stretched for several hundred yards. A little distance from the breastwork, the shadow of Black Rifle came forward.

     #50986—Leveled Texts for Classic Fiction: Historical Fiction

"Nothing yet?" asked the hunter.

"Nothing so far, but there are three or four good men with me among the stumps, though not a warrior has yet appeared. I suppose they know we'll be on watch here, and it's not worth taking so great a risk."

They advanced to the far edge of the stump region and crouched there, as the night was now quite dark, the moon almost hidden, the stars but few, and the forest a solid black line before them.

"Why can't Tayoga use his ears?" said Grosvenor. "He'll hear them even a mile away."

"A little farther on and he will," replied Willet, "but we, in our turn, don't dare to go deep into the forest."

A hundred yards more and the Tayoga, the Onondaga, put his ear to the ground, but it was a long time before he announced anything.

"I hear footsteps fairly near to us," he said at last, "and I think they are those of warriors. They would be more cautious, but they do not believe we are outside the line of logs. Yes, they are warriors, all warriors, because there is no jingle of metal such as the French have on their coats or belts. They are going to take a look at our position and are about to pass now to our right. I also hear other steps, but farther away, on our left, and I think they are the steps of those Frenchmen."

"Likely De Courcelles and Jumonville who want also to look us over," said Willet.

"There is another and larger force coming directly toward us," continued the Onondaga, "and I think it includes both the French and the warriors. This may be the attack and perhaps it would be better for us to fall back."

Element Focus: Plot

What sequel could result from this passage?

Excerpt from

Kidnapped

by Robert L. Stevenson

I had guessed it a long while ago. It is one thing to guess. It is another to know. I sat stunned with my good fortune. I could not believe that the same poor lad who had walked from Ettrick Forest not two days ago was now rich. He now had a house and broad lands, and might ride his horse tomorrow. All these pleasant things and more were in my mind. I sat staring out the inn window. I paid no attention to what I saw. I remember that I saw Captain Hoseason. He was down on the pier among his seamen. He was speaking with some authority. Then he came marching back towards the house. He was not clumsy like a sailor. He carried his fine, tall figure with a manly bearing. He had the same sober, grave expression on his face. I wondered if it was possible that Ransome's stories could be true. I half disbelieved his stories. They did not fit with the captain's looks. But indeed, the captain was not as good as I thought. He was not as bad as Ransome thought. For, in fact, he was two men. He left the better man behind once on board his vessel.

Then I heard my uncle calling me. I found the pair in the road together. The captain spoke to me. He spoke words that were flattering to a young lad. He treated me as an equal.

"Sir," said he, "Mr. Balfour tells me great things of you. I like your looks. I wish I was to stay longer here. We might become better friends. But we will make the most of our time. Ye shall come on board my brig for half an hour. Come till the ebb sets. Drink a bowl with me."

I longed to see the inside of a ship. But I was not going to put myself in danger. I told him that my uncle and I had an appointment with a lawyer.

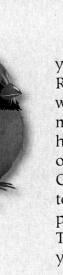

"Ay, ay," said he, "he told me that. But, the boat will put you ashore at the town pier. That is but a short way from Rankeillor's house." And here he suddenly leaned down. He whispered in my ear: "Take care of the old tod. He means mischief. Come aboard till I can get a word with ye." And then he passed his arm through mine. He continued aloud. He set off towards his boat: "But, come, what can I bring ye from the Carolinas? Any friend of Mr. Balfour's can command. A roll of tobacco? Indian feather-work? A skin of a wild beast? A stone pipe? The mockingbird that mews for all the world like a cat? The cardinal bird that is as red as blood? Take your pick. Say your pleasure."

By this time we were at the boat. The captain helped me on the boat. I did not dream of hanging back. I thought (the poor fool!) that I had found a good friend and helper. I was happy to see the ship. Soon we were all on board. The boat sailed from the pier. It began to move over the waters. I felt pleasure in this new movement and surprise at our low position. I saw the shores appear, and the growing bigness of the brig as we drew near to it. I could hardly understand what the captain said. I must have answered him without thinking.

Soon we were alongside. I stared at the ship's height. There was a strong humming. It was the tide against its sides. I could hear the pleasant cries of the seamen at their work. Hoseason said he and I must go aboard first. He ordered a tackle from the main-yard. In this I was lifted into the air. I was set down again on the deck. The captain waited for me. He instantly slipped his arm back under mine. There I stood some while. I was a little dizzy. It was unsteady all around me. Perhaps I was a little afraid. Yet I was very pleased with these strange sights. The captain pointed out the strangest sights. He told me their names and uses.

Element Focus: Plot

What words or phrases does the author use to build suspense so that the reader is eager to find out what happens next?

Kidnapped

by Robert L. Stevenson

Of course, I had guessed it a long while ago. It is one thing to guess, another to know. I sat stunned with my good fortune. It was hard to believe that the same poor lad who had trudged in the dust from Ettrick Forest not two days ago was now one of the rich of the earth. That he had a house and broad lands, and might mount his horse tomorrow. All these pleasant things, and a thousand others, crowded into my mind. I sat staring before me out of the inn window. I was paying no attention to what I saw. I remember that my eye spotted Captain Hoseason down on the pier among his seamen. He was speaking with some authority. And presently he came marching back towards the house. He had no mark of a sailor's clumsiness. He was carrying his fine, tall figure with a manly bearing. He still had the same sober, grave expression on his face. I wondered if it was possible that Ransome's stories could be true, and half disbelieved them. They did not fit with the man's looks. But indeed, he was not so good as I supposed thought, nor quite so bad as Ransome thought. For, in fact, he was two men. He left the better man behind when he set foot on board his vessel.

The next thing, I heard my uncle calling me. I found the pair in the road together. It was the captain who spoke to me. He had an air (very flattering to a young lad) of grave equality.

"Sir," said he, "Mr. Balfour tells me great things of you. For my own part, I like your looks. I wish I was to stay longer here that we might become better friends. But we will make the most of our time. Ye shall come on board my brig for half an hour, till the ebb sets. Drink a bowl with me."

Now, I longed to see the inside of a ship more than words can tell. Yet I was not going to put myself in danger. I told him that my uncle and I had an appointment with a lawyer.

"Ay, ay," said he, "he informed me of that. But, the boat will set ye ashore at the town pier. That is but a penny stonecast from Rankeillor's house." And here he suddenly leaned down. He whispered in my ear: "Take care of the old tod. He means mischief. Come aboard till I can get a word with ye." And then he put his arm through mine. He continued aloud. He set off towards his boat: "But, come, what can I bring ye from the Carolinas? Any friend of Mr. Balfour's can command. A roll of tobacco? Indian feather-work? A skin of a wild beast? A stone pipe? The mockingbird that mews for all the world like a cat? The cardinal bird that is as red as blood? Take your pick and say your pleasure."

By this time, we were at the boat-side. He was handing me in. I did not dream of hanging back. I thought (the poor fool!) that I had found a good friend and helper. I was happy to see the ship. Soon we were all set in our places. The boat was thrust off from the pier. It began to move over the waters. What with my pleasure in this new movement and my surprise at our low position, and the appearance of the shores, and the growing bigness of the brig as we drew near to it, I could hardly understand what the captain said. I must have answered him at random.

As soon as we were alongside (where I sat fairly gaping at the ship's height, the strong humming of the tide against its sides, and the pleasant cries of the seamen at their work), Hoseason, declaring that he and I must be the first aboard, ordered a tackle to be sent down from the main-yard. In this, I was whipped into the air and set down again on the deck. The captain stood ready waiting for me. He instantly slipped back his arm under mine. There I stood some while. I was a little dizzy with the unsteadiness of all around me. Perhaps I was a little afraid, and yet vastly pleased with these strange sights. The captain meanwhile pointing out the strangest sights, and telling me their names and uses.

Element Focus: Plot

What clues in the passage let the reader know that something bad is going to happen?

Excerpt from

Kidnapped

by Robert L. Stevenson

Of course, I had guessed it a long while ago; but it is one thing to guess, another to know; and I sat stunned with my good fortune, and could scarce grow to believe that the same poor lad who had trudged in the dust from Ettrick Forest not two days ago, was now one of the rich of the earth, and had a house and broad lands, and might mount his horse tomorrow. All these pleasant things, and a thousand others, crowded into my mind, as I sat staring before me out of the inn window, and paying no heed to what I saw; only I remember that my eye lighted on Captain Hoseason down on the pier among his seamen, and speaking with some authority. And presently he came marching back towards the house, with no mark of a sailor's clumsiness, but carrying his fine, tall figure with a manly bearing, and still with the same sober, grave expression on his face. I wondered if it was possible that Ransome's stories could be true, and half disbelieved them; they fitted so ill with the man's looks. But indeed, he was neither so good as I supposed him, nor quite so bad as Ransome did; for, in fact, he was two men, and left the better one behind as soon as he set foot on board his vessel.

The next thing, I heard my uncle calling me, and found the pair in the road together. It was the captain who addressed me, and that with an air (very flattering to a young lad) of grave equality.

"Sir," said he, "Mr. Balfour tells me great things of you; and for my own part, I like your looks. I wish I was for longer here, that we might make the better friends; but we'll make the most of what we have. Ye shall come on board my brig for half an hour, till the ebb sets, and drink a bowl with me."

Now, I longed to see the inside of a ship more than words can tell; but I was not going to put myself in jeopardy, and I told him my uncle and I had an appointment with a lawyer.

"Ay, ay," said he, "he passed me word of that. But, ye see, the boat'll set ye ashore at the town pier, and that's but a penny stonecast from Rankeillor's house." And here he suddenly leaned down and whispered in my ear: "Take care of the old tod; he means mischief. Come aboard till I can get a word with ye." And then, passing his arm through mine, he continued aloud, as he set off towards his boat: "But, come, what can I bring ye from the Carolinas? Any friend of Mr. Balfour's can command. A roll of tobacco? Indian feather-work? A skin of a wild beast? A stone pipe? The mocking-bird that mews for all the world like a cat? The cardinal bird that is as red as blood?—take your pick and say your pleasure."

By this time we were at the boat-side, and he was handing me in. I did not dream of hanging back; I thought (the poor fool!) that I had found a good friend and helper, and I was rejoiced to see the ship. As soon as we were all set in our places, the boat was thrust off from the pier and began to move over the waters: and what with my pleasure in this new movement and my surprise at our low position, and the appearance of the shores, and the growing bigness of the brig as we drew near to it, I could hardly understand what the captain said, and must have answered him at random.

As soon as we were alongside (where I sat fairly gaping at the ship's height, the strong humming of the tide against its sides, and the pleasant cries of the seamen at their work) Hoseason, declaring that he and I must be the first aboard, ordered a tackle to be sent down from the main-yard. In this I was whipped into the air and set down again on the deck, where the captain stood ready waiting for me, and instantly slipped back his arm under mine. There I stood some while, a little dizzy with the unsteadiness of all around me, perhaps a little afraid, and yet vastly pleased with these strange sights; the captain meanwhile pointing out the strangest, and telling me their names and uses.

Element Focus: Plot

When does the character first understand that something is wrong about this innocent boat ride?

#50986—Leveled Texts for Classic Fiction: Historical Fiction

Excerpt from

Kidnapped

by Robert L. Stevenson

Of course, I had guessed it a long while ago; but it is one thing to guess, another to know; and I sat stunned with my good fortune, and could scarce grow to believe that the same poor lad who had trudged in the dust from Ettrick Forest not two days ago, was now one of the rich of the earth, and had a house and broad lands, and might mount his horse tomorrow. All these pleasant things, and a thousand others, crowded into my mind, as I sat staring before me out of the inn window, and paying no heed to what I saw; only I remember that my eye lighted on Captain Hoseason down on the pier among his seamen, and speaking with some authority. And presently he came marching back towards the house, with no mark of a sailor's clumsiness, but carrying his fine, tall figure with a manly bearing, and still with the same sober, grave expression on his face. I wondered if it was possible that Ransome's stories could be true, and half disbelieved them; they fitted so ill with the man's looks. But indeed, he was neither so good as I supposed him, nor quite so bad as Ransome did; for, in fact, he was two men, and left the better one behind as soon as he set foot on board his vessel.

The next thing, I heard my uncle calling me, and found the pair in the road together. It was the captain who addressed me, and that with an air (very flattering to a young lad) of grave equality.

"Sir," said he, "Mr. Balfour tells me great things of you; and for my own part, I like your looks. I wish I was for longer here, that we might make the better friends; but we'll make the most of what we have. Ye shall come on board my brig for half an hour, till the ebb sets, and drink a bowl with me."

Now, I longed to see the inside of a ship more than words can tell, but I was not going to put myself in jeopardy, and I told him that my uncle and I had an appointment with a lawyer.

"Ay, ay," said he, "he passed me word of that. But, ye see, the boat'll set ye ashore at the town pier, and that's but a penny stonecast from Rankeillor's house." And here he suddenly leaned down and whispered in my ear: "Take care of the old tod because he means mischief. Come aboard till I can get a word with ye." And then, passing his arm through mine, he continued aloud, as he set off towards his boat: "But, come, what can I bring ye from the Carolinas? Any friend of Mr. Balfour's can command. A roll of tobacco, Indian feather-work, a skin of a wild beast, a stone pipe, the mockingbird that mews for all the world like a cat, the cardinal bird that is as red as blood? Take your pick and say your pleasure."

By this time, we were at the boat-side, and he was handing me in. I did not dream of hanging back; I thought (the poor fool!) that I had found a good friend and helper, and I was rejoiced to see the ship. As soon as we were all set in our places, the boat was thrust off from the pier and began to move over the waters: and what with my pleasure in this new movement and my surprise at our low position, and the appearance of the shores, and the growing bigness of the brig as we drew near to it, I could hardly understand what the captain said, and must have answered him at random.

As soon as we were alongside (where I sat fairly gaping at the ship's height, the strong humming of the tide against its sides, and the pleasant cries of the seamen at their work), Hoseason, declaring that he and I must be the first aboard, ordered a tackle to be sent down from the main-yard. In this, I was whipped into the air and set down again on the deck, where the captain stood ready waiting for me, and instantly slipped back his arm under mine. There I stood some while, a little dizzy with the unsteadiness of all around me, perhaps a little afraid, and yet vastly pleased with these strange sights; the captain meanwhile pointing out the strangest, and telling me their names and uses.

Element Focus: Plot

Predict what will happen to the young boy in this story.

Excerpt from

In the Days of the Guild

by Louise Lamprey

The road would not really be called a road today. It was a track. It was trodden out about halfway up the slope of the valley. Now and then it ran along the top of the long, low hills. The hills have been called downs as long as man has been around them. Sometimes it would make a sharp twist to cross the shallows of a stream. There were scarcely any bridges in the country. In some places, it was wide enough for a squad. Yet it was faintly marked. In others it was bitten deep into the hillside. It was so narrow that three men could hardly have gone abreast upon it. But it did not need to be anything more than a trail. No wagons went that way. There were only travelers afoot or a-horseback. Some times there would be wayfarers all along the road. They would travel from early in the morning until sunset. They would even be found camping by the wayside. At other times of the year, one might walk for hours upon it. You might meet nobody at all. Robert had been sitting where he was for about three hours. He had walked between four and five miles to reach the road. He had a woolpack on his shoulder. He had risen before the sun that morning. Now he began to wonder if the wool-merchants had already gone by. It was late in the season. Perhaps they had. Then there was hardly any hope of sending the wool to market this year.

But worry never worked aught, as the saying is. People who take care of sheep seem to worry less than others. There are many things that they cannot change. They are kept busy attending to their flocks. Robert did not intend to be called Hob anymore. He took from his pouch some coarse bread and cheese. He began munching it. By the sun, it was the dinner-hour. It was around nine o'clock. Meanwhile, he checked the silver penny. It was in the corner of the pouch. The pouch hung at his girdle. It served him for a pocket. He checked that it was safe. It was. It was about the size of a modern halfpenny. It had a cross on one side. A penny such as this could be cut in quarters. Each piece could be passed as a coin.

The last bit of bread and cheese vanished. Then came the jingle-jangle of strings of bells on the necks of pack horses. They came from far away over the fern. A few minutes later, the shaggy head and neck of the leader came in sight. They were strong horses. Yet they were not very big. They were not built for racing. They were quick walkers. They could travel over rough country at a very good pace. It did not matter if they were loaded heavily with packs of wool. Robert stood up. His heart was beating fast. He had never seen them so close before. The merchants were laughing and talking. They seemed to be in a good humor. He hoped very much that they would speak to him.

"Ho!" said the one who rode nearest to him. "Here is another, as I live. Did you grow out of the ground? Have your roots like the rest of them? Are you a bumpkin?"

Robert bowed. He was mad. Yet this was no time to answer back. "I have wool to sell. So, please you," he said. "Are you in need of a horse-boy? I would work my passage to London."

The man who had spoken frowned. He pulled at his beard. The leader had been talking to someone behind him. Now he turned his face toward Robert. He was a kindly-looking, ruddy-cheeked old fellow. He had eyes as sharp as the stars on a clear winter night.

Element Focus: Plot

How does the leader of the merchants treat Robert as he talks to the group? Why would he treat him this way?

In the Days of the Guild

by Louise Lamprey

The road would not really be called a road today. It was a track. It was trodden out about halfway up the slope of the valley in some parts of it. Now and then it ran along the top of the long, low hills. The hills have been called downs as long as the memory of man holds a trace of them. Sometimes it would make a sharp twist to cross the shallows of a stream. There were scarcely any bridges in the country. In some places, it was wide enough for a regiment, but faintly marked. In others, it was bitten deep into the hillside. It was so narrow that three men could hardly have gone abreast upon it. But it did not need to be anything more than a trail, or bridle-path. No wagons went that way. There were only travelers afoot or a-horseback. At some seasons, there would be wayfarers all along the road from early in the morning until sunset. They would even be found camping by the wayside. At other times of the year, one might walk for hours upon it and meet nobody at all. Robert had been sitting where he was for about three hours. He had walked between four and five miles to reach the road. He had a woolpack on his shoulder. He had risen before the sun that morning. Now he began to wonder if the wool-merchants had already gone by. It was late in the season. If they had, there was hardly any hope of sending the wool to market this year.

But worry never worked aught, as the saying is. People who take care of sheep seem to worry less than others. There are many things that they cannot change. They are kept busy attending to their flocks. Robert did not intend to be called Hob anymore. He took from his pouch some coarse bread and cheese and began munching it. By the sun, it was the dinner-hour. It was around nine o'clock. Meanwhile, he checked the silver penny in the corner of the pouch. The pouch hung at his girdle and served him for a pocket. He checked that it was safe. It was. It was about the size of a modern halfpenny and had a cross on one side. A penny such as this could be cut in quarters. Each piece could be passed as a coin.

Just as the last bit of bread and cheese vanished, there came, from far away over the fern, the jingle-jangle of strings of bells on the necks of pack-horses. A few minutes later, the shaggy head and neck of the leader came in sight. They were strong, not very big horses. While they were not built for racing, they were quick walkers. They could travel over rough country at a very good pace, even when they were loaded heavily with packs of wool. Robert stood up, his heart beating fast. He had never seen them so close before. The merchants were laughing and talking and seemed to be in a good humor. He hoped very much that they would speak to him.

"Ho!" said the one who rode nearest to him. "Here's another, as I live. Did you grow out of the ground? Have your roots like the rest of them, bumpkin?"

Robert bowed. He was rather angry. Yet this was no time to answer back. "I have wool to sell, so please you," he said. "If you be in need of a horse-boy, I would work my passage to London."

The man who had spoken frowned and pulled at his beard. The leader, who had been talking to someone behind him, now turned his face toward Robert. He was a kindly-looking, ruddy-cheeked old fellow. He had eyes as sharp as the stars on a winter night that is clear.

Element Focus: Plot

In what ways does Robert act brave as he tries to sell his wool to the merchants?

#50986—*Leveled Texts for Classic Fiction: Historical Fiction*   © *Shell Education*

In the Days of the Guild

by Louise Lamprey

The road would not really be called a road today. It was a track. It was trodden out about halfway up the slope of the valley in some parts of it. Now and then it ran along the top of the long, low hills. The hills have been called downs as long as the memory of man holds a trace of them. Sometimes it would make a sharp twist to cross the shallows of a stream. There were scarcely any bridges in the country. In some places, it was wide enough for a regiment, but faintly marked. In others, it was bitten deep into the hillside. It was so constricted that three men could hardly have gone abreast upon it. But it did not need to be anything more than a trail, or bridle-path. No wagons went that way. There were only travelers afoot or a-horseback. At some seasons, there would be wayfarers all along the road from early in the morning until sunset. They would even be found camping by the wayside. At other times of the year, one might walk for hours upon it and meet nobody at all. Robert had been sitting where he was for about three hours. He had walked between four and five miles to reach the road. He had a woolpack on his shoulder. He had risen before the sun that morning. Now he began to wonder if the wool-merchants had already gone by. It was late in the season. If they had, there was hardly any hope of sending the wool to market this year.

But worry never worked aught, as the saying is, and people who take care of sheep seem to worry less than others; there are many things that they cannot change, and they are kept busy attending to their flocks. Robert, who did not intend to be called Hob anymore, took from his pouch some coarse bread and cheese and began munching it, for by the sun it was the dinner-hour—nine o'clock. Meanwhile, he made sure that the silver penny in the corner of the pouch, which hung at his girdle and served him for a pocket, was safe. It was. It was about the size of a modern halfpenny and had a cross on one side. A penny such as this could be cut in quarters, and each portion passed as a coin.

Just as the last bit of bread and cheese vanished, there came, from far away over the fern, the jingle-jangle of strings of bells on the necks of pack-horses. A few minutes later, the shaggy head and neck of the leader came in sight. They were strong, not very big horses; and while they were not built for racing, they were quick walkers. They could travel over rough country at a very good pace, even when, as they now were, loaded heavily with packs of wool. Robert stood up, his heart beating fast: He had never seen them so close before. The merchants were laughing and talking and seemed to be in a good humor, and he hoped very much that they would speak to him.

"Ho!" said the one who rode nearest to him, "here's another, as I live. Did you grow out of the ground, and have your roots like the rest of them, bumpkin?"

Robert bowed; he was rather angry, but this was no time to answer back. "I have wool to sell, so please you," he said, "and—if you be in need of a horse-boy, I would work my passage to London."

The man who had spoken frowned and pulled at his beard, but the leader, who had been talking to someone behind him, now turned his face toward Robert. He was a kindly-looking, ruddy-cheeked old fellow, with eyes as sharp as the stars on a winter night that is clear.

Element Focus: Plot

What does Robert's behavior tell you about how difficult it may have been for him to sell wool?

In the Days of the Guild

by Louise Lamprey

The road would not really be called a road today. It was a track, trodden out about half way up the slope of the valley in some parts of it, and now and then running along the top of the long, low hills that have been called downs as long as the memory of man holds a trace of them. Sometimes it would make a sharp twist to cross the shallows of a stream, for there were scarcely any bridges in the country. In some places it was wide enough for a regiment, and but faintly marked; in others it was bitten deep into the hillside and so narrow that three men could hardly have gone abreast upon it. But it did not need to be anything more than a trail, or bridle-path, because no wagons went that way,—only travelers afoot or a-horseback. At some seasons there would be wayfarers all along the road from early in the morning until sunset, and they would even be found camping by the wayside; at other times of the year one might walk for hours upon it and meet nobody at all. Robert had been sitting where he was for about three hours; and he had walked between four and five miles, woolpack on his shoulder, before he reached the road; he had risen before the sun that morning. Now he began to wonder if the wool-merchants had already gone by. It was late in the season, and if they had, there was hardly any hope of sending the wool to market this year.

But worry never worked aught, as the saying is, and people who take care of sheep seem to worry less than others; there are many things that they cannot change, and they are kept busy attending to their flocks. Robert, who did not intend to be called Hob any more, took from his pouch some coarse bread and cheese and began munching it, for by the sun it was the dinner-hour—nine o'clock. Meanwhile he made sure that the silver penny in the corner of the pouch, which hung at his girdle and served him for a pocket, was safe. It was. It was about the size of a modern halfpenny and had a cross on one side. A penny such as this could be cut in quarters, and each piece passed as a coin.

Just as the last bit of bread and cheese vanished there came, from far away over the fern, the jingle-jangle of strings of bells on the necks of pack-horses. A few minutes later the shaggy head and neck of the leader came in sight. They were strong, not very big horses; and while they were not built for racing, they were quick walkers. They could travel over rough country at a very good pace, even when, as they now were, loaded heavily with packs of wool. Robert stood up, his heart beating fast: he had never seen them so close before. The merchants were laughing and talking and seemed to be in a good humor, and he hoped very much that they would communicate to him.

"Ho!" said the one who rode nearest to him, "here's another, as I live. Did you grow out of the ground, and have your roots like the rest of them, bumpkin?"

Robert bowed; he was rather angry, but this was no time to answer back. "I have wool to sell, so please you," he said, "and—if you be in need of a horse-boy, I would work my passage to London."

The man who had spoken frowned and pulled at his beard, but the leader, who had been talking to some one behind him, now turned his face toward Robert. He was a kindly-looking, ruddy-cheeked old fellow, with eyes as sharp as the stars on a winter night that is clear.

Element Focus: Plot

What is Robert waiting for, and why is it so important to catch this group of people as they travel by? What would you do if you were in Robert's position?

Excerpt from

Anne of Green Gables

by Lucy Maud Montgomery

He reached Bright River. There was no sign of any train. He thought he was too early. He tied his horse. He went over to the station house. The long platform was almost deserted. The only living creature in sight was a girl. She was sitting on a pile of stones. Matthew barely noted that it *was* a girl. He sidled past her. He moved as quickly as possible. He did not look at her. She was tense rigid. She was sitting there. She was waiting for something or somebody. Sitting and waiting was all she could do just then.

Matthew met the stationmaster. He was locking up the ticket office. He was going home for supper. Matthew asked him if the five-thirty train would soon be along.

"The five-thirty train has been in. It was gone half an hour ago," answered that brisk official. "There was a passenger dropped off for you. It was a little girl. She is sitting out there. She is on the stones. I asked her to go into the ladies' waiting room. She said she preferred to stay outside. 'There was more scope for imagination,' she said. She is a case. I should say."

"I am not expecting a girl," said Matthew blankly. "It is a boy I have come for. He should be here. Mrs. Alexander Spencer was to bring him over. They were coming from Nova Scotia for me."

The stationmaster whistled.

"Guess there is some mistake," he said. "Mrs. Spencer came off the train. She was with that girl. She gave her into my charge. Said you and your sister were adopting her. Getting her from an orphan home. She said that you would be along for her presently. That is all I know about it. I have not got any more orphans hidden hereabouts."

"I do not understand," said Matthew weakly. He wished Marilla was at hand. He wanted her to cope with the problem.

"You better question the girl," said the stationmaster carelessly. "I dare say she will be able to explain. She has got a tongue of her own. That is certain. Maybe they were out of boys of the brand you wanted."

The station master walked jauntily away. He was hungry. Matthew was left alone to do something. It was hard for him. It was harder than facing a lion in its den. He had to walk up to a girl. She was a strange girl. She was an orphan girl. He had to ask her why she was not a boy. Matthew groaned in spirit. He turned about. He shuffled down the platform. He moved towards the girl.

She had been watching him. She had seen him since he had passed her. She had her eyes on him now. Matthew was not looking at her. He would not have seen what she was really like. Anyone would have seen a child of about eleven. She was dressed in a very short dress. It was very tight. It was also very ugly. It was of yellowish-gray wincey. She wore a faded brown sailor hat. Beneath the hat were two braids. She had very thick red hair. The braids were extending down her back. Her face was small. It was white and thin. It was also much freckled. Her mouth was large. So were her eyes. The eyes looked green in some lights and moods. They looked gray in others.

An observer might have seen something. Her chin was pointed and pronounced. Her eyes were big. They were full of spirit and energy. Her mouth was sweet-lipped. It was expressive. Her forehead was broad and full. No commonplace soul was in the body of this stray child. So why was Matthew Cuthbert so afraid of her?

Element Focus: Plot

What lessons could this story teach us?

#50986—Leveled Texts for Classic Fiction: Historical Fiction   © *Shell Education*

Excerpt from

Anne of Green Gables

by Lucy Maud Montgomery

He reached Bright River. There was no sign of any train. He thought he was too early. He tied his horse. The horse stayed in the yard of the small Bright River hotel. He went over to the station house. The long platform was almost deserted. The only living creature in sight was a girl. She was sitting on a pile of shingles. She was at the extreme end. Matthew barely noted that it was a girl. He sidled past her. He moved as quickly as possible. He did not look at her. Had he looked, he could hardly have failed to notice her. She had a tense rigidity and expectation in her attitude and expression. She was sitting there waiting for something or somebody. Sitting and waiting was all she could do just then. So she sat and waited with all her might and main.

Matthew met the stationmaster. He was preparing to lock up the ticket office. He was going home for supper. Matthew asked him if the five-thirty train would soon be along.

"The five-thirty train has been in. It was gone half an hour ago," answered that brisk official. "But there was a passenger dropped off for you. It was a little girl. She is sitting out there on the shingles. I asked her to go into the ladies' waiting room. She informed me gravely that she preferred to stay outside. 'There was more scope for imagination,' she said. She is a case, I should say."

"I am not expecting a girl," said Matthew blankly. "It is a boy I have come for. He should be here. Mrs. Alexander Spencer was to bring him over from Nova Scotia for me."

The stationmaster whistled.

"Guess there is some mistake," he said. "Mrs. Spencer came off the train with that girl. She gave her into my charge. Said you and your sister were adopting her from an orphan asylum. She said that you would be along for her presently. That is all I know about it. I have not got any more orphans concealed hereabouts."

"I do not understand," said Matthew helplessly. He was wishing that Marilla was at hand. He wanted her to cope with the situation.

"You better question the girl," said the stationmaster carelessly. "I dare say she will be able to explain. She has got a tongue of her own. That is certain. Maybe they were out of boys of the brand you wanted."

The stationmaster walked jauntily away. He was hungry. The unfortunate Matthew was left alone to do something. It was harder for him than bearding a lion in its den. He had to walk up to a girl. She was a strange girl. She was an orphan girl. He had to demand of her why she was not a boy. Matthew groaned in spirit. He turned about. He shuffled gently down the platform towards her.

She had been watching him ever since he had passed her. She had her eyes on him now. Matthew was not looking at her. He would not have seen what she was really like if he had been. Yet an ordinary observer would have seen a child of about eleven. She was garbed in a very short dress. It was very tight. It was also very ugly of yellowish-gray wincey. She wore a faded brown sailor hat. Beneath the hat were two braids of very thick, decidedly red hair. The braids were extending down her back. Her face was small, white, and thin. It was also much freckled. Her mouth was large. So were her eyes. The eyes looked green in some lights and moods and gray in others.

An extraordinary observer might have seen that the chin was very pointed and pronounced. That the big eyes were full of spirit and vivacity. That the mouth was sweet-lipped and expressive. That the forehead was broad and full. It was easy to conclude that no commonplace soul inhabited the body of this stray child of whom shy Matthew Cuthbert was so afraid.

Element Focus: Plot

What do you think might happen to this girl?

Excerpt from

Anne of Green Gables

by Lucy Maud Montgomery

When he reached Bright River there was no sign of any train. He thought he was too early. He tied his horse in the yard of the small Bright River hotel and went over to the station house. The long platform was almost deserted. The only living creature in sight was a girl who was sitting on a pile of shingles at the extreme end. Matthew, barely noting that it was a girl, sidled past her as quickly as possible without looking at her. Had he looked he could hardly have failed to notice the tense rigidity and expectation of her attitude and expression. She was sitting there waiting for something or somebody. Since sitting and waiting was the only thing to do just then, she sat and waited with all her might and main.

Matthew encountered the stationmaster locking up the ticket office preparatory to go home for supper. He asked him if the five-thirty train would soon be along.

"The five-thirty train has been in and gone half an hour ago," answered that brisk official. "But there was a passenger dropped off for you. It was a little girl. She is sitting out there on the shingles. I asked her to go into the ladies' waiting room. She informed me gravely that she preferred to stay outside. 'There was more scope for imagination,' she said. She is a case, I should say."

"I am not expecting a girl," said Matthew blankly. "It is a boy I have come for. He should be here. Mrs. Alexander Spencer was to bring him over from Nova Scotia for me."

The stationmaster whistled.

"Guess there's some mistake," he said. "Mrs. Spencer came off the train with that girl and gave her into my charge. Said you and your sister were adopting her from an orphan asylum and that you would be along for her presently. That is all I know about it. I haven't got any more orphans concealed hereabouts."

"I don't understand," said Matthew helplessly. He was wishing that Marilla was at hand to cope with the situation.

"Well, you'd better question the girl," said the stationmaster carelessly. "I dare say she will be able to explain. She's got a tongue of her own. That is certain. Maybe they were out of boys of the brand you wanted."

The stationmaster walked jauntily away, being hungry. The unfortunate Matthew was left alone to do that which was harder for him than bearding a lion in its den. He had to walk up to a girl. She was a strange girl. She was an orphan girl. He had to demand of her why she wasn't a boy. Matthew groaned in spirit as he turned about. He shuffled gently down the platform towards her.

She had been watching him ever since he had passed her. She had her eyes on him now. Matthew was not looking at her. He would not have seen what she was really like if he had been. Yet an ordinary observer would have seen a child of about eleven. She was garbed in a very short, very tight, very ugly dress of yellowish-gray wincey. She wore a faded brown sailor hat. Beneath the hat, extending down her back, were two braids of very thick, decidedly red hair. Her face was small, white, and thin, also much freckled; her mouth was large and so were her eyes, which looked green in some lights and moods and gray in others.

So far, the ordinary observer; an extraordinary observer might have seen that the chin was very pointed and pronounced; that the big eyes were full of spirit and vivacity; that the mouth was sweet-lipped and expressive; that the forehead was broad and full; in short, our discerning extraordinary observer might have concluded that no commonplace soul inhabited the body of this stray woman-child of whom shy Matthew Cuthbert was so ludicrously afraid.

Element Focus: Plot

How does Matthew handle the surprising situation he is in? How might you handle the situation?

Anne of Green Gables

by Lucy Maud Montgomery

When he reached Bright River there was no sign of any train; he thought he was too early, so he tied his horse in the yard of the small Bright River hotel and went over to the station house. The long platform was almost deserted; the only living creature in sight being a girl who was sitting on a pile of shingles at the extreme end. Matthew, barely noting that it was a girl, sidled past her as quickly as possible without looking at her. Had he looked he could hardly have failed to notice the tense rigidity and expectation of her attitude and expression. She was sitting there waiting for something or somebody and, since sitting and waiting was the only thing to do just then, she sat and waited with all her might and main.

Matthew encountered the stationmaster locking up the ticket office preparatory to going home for supper, and asked him if the five-thirty train would soon be along.

"The five-thirty train has been in and gone half an hour ago," answered that brisk official. "But there was a passenger dropped off for you—a little girl. She's sitting out there on the shingles. I asked her to go into the ladies' waiting room, but she informed me gravely that she preferred to stay outside. 'There was more scope for imagination,' she said. She's a case, I should say."

"I'm not expecting a girl," said Matthew blankly. "It's a boy I've come for. He should be here. Mrs. Alexander Spencer was to bring him over from Nova Scotia for me."

The stationmaster whistled.

"Guess there's some mistake," he said. "Mrs. Spencer came off the train with that girl and gave her into my charge. Said you and your sister were adopting her from an orphan asylum and that you would be along for her presently. That's all I know about it—and I haven't got any more orphans concealed hereabouts."

"I don't understand," said Matthew helplessly, wishing that Marilla was at hand to cope with the situation.

"Well, you'd better question the girl," said the stationmaster carelessly. "I dare say she'll be able to explain—she's got a tongue of her own, that's certain. Maybe they were out of boys of the brand you wanted."

He walked jauntily away, being hungry, and the unfortunate Matthew was left to do that which was harder for him than bearding a lion in its den—walk up to a girl—a strange girl—an orphan girl—and demand of her why she wasn't a boy. Matthew groaned in spirit as he turned about and shuffled gently down the platform towards her.

She had been watching him ever since he had passed her and she had her eyes on him now. Matthew was not looking at her and would not have seen what she was really like if he had been, but an ordinary observer would have seen this: A child of about eleven, garbed in a very short, very tight, very ugly dress of yellowish-gray wincey. She wore a faded brown sailor hat and beneath the hat, extending down her back, were two braids of very thick, decidedly red hair. Her face was small, white and thin, also much freckled; her mouth was large and so were her eyes, which looked green in some lights and moods and gray in others.

So far, the ordinary observer; an extraordinary observer might have seen that the chin was very pointed and pronounced; that the big eyes were full of spirit and vivacity; that the mouth was sweet-lipped and expressive; that the forehead was broad and full; in short, our discerning extraordinary observer might have concluded that no commonplace soul inhabited the body of this stray woman-child of whom shy Matthew Cuthbert was so ludicrously afraid.

Element Focus: Plot

How is this story similar to other stories you have read?

#50986—*Leveled Texts for Classic Fiction: Historical Fiction*   © *Shell Education*

The Puritan Twins

by Lucy Fitch Perkins

Daniel was standing on the deck. He was on the Lucy Ann. He was drinking in the fresh salt breeze. He was watching the shores. The boat passed between Charlestown and Boston. It dropped anchor in the harbor. They were to set the Captain's lobster-pots. All day they sailed. They went past rocky islands. They saw picturesque headlands. The Captain was at the tiller. He was skillfully keeping the vessel to the course. At the same time, he was spinning yarns to Daniel and his father. He talked about adventures. These events had happened him at various points along the coast. He had caught a giant lobster. This was at Governor's Island. He had been all but wrecked in a fog. This was off Thompson's Island.

"Ye see that point of land," he said. He was waving his hand. He pointed toward a rocky promontory. It extended far out into the bay. "That is Squantum. Miles Standish of Plymouth named it. It was named after an Indian. He was a good friend of the Colony in the early days. See right off there? I was overhauled by a French privateer once. 'Privateer' is a polite name. It means a pirate ship. She was loaded with molasses and indigo. She was from the West Indies. I had a cargo of beaver-skins. Her sailors was mostly roarin' drunk at the time. Or else it would have been the end of Thomas Sanders. But my boat was smaller and quicker than theirs. I know these waters so well. I was able to give them the slip. I got out into open sea. Here I be! Those were the days!"

The Captain heaved a heavy sigh. He thought of the lost joys of youth. He was silent for a moment. Then his eyes twinkled. He began another story. "One day, we was skirtin' the shores. We were near Martha's Vineyard," he said. "We were followed by a shark. There is nothing a sailor hates worse than a shark. For good reasons. They are the pirates of the deep. That is what they are. They will follow a vessel for days. They snap up whatever the cook throws out. They are hoping somebody will fall overboard. That would give them a full meal. There was a sailor aboard on that voyage. He had a special grudge against sharks. He had been all but et up by one once. He allowed this was his chance to get even. So he let out a hook. It was baited. It had a whole pound of salt pork. The shark gobbled it down instanter. He ate hook and all. They hauled him up the ship's side. Then that sailor let himself down over the rails by a rope. He cut a hole in the shark's gullet. That is whatever they call the pouch the critter carries his supplies in. He took out the pork. Then he dropped him back in the water. He threw the pork in after him. That shark sighted the pork. It was bobbing 'round in the water. He swallowed it again. Of course it dropped right out. It went through the hole in his gullet. By jolly! As long as we could see him, that shark was continuing to swallow. He ate that piece of pork over and over again. I do not know any animal who got more pleasure out of his rations. That shark enjoyed that pound of pork. I believe in bein' kind to dumb critters," he finished. "I reckon the shark is about the dumbdest there is. Anyhow that one surely did die happy." Here the Captain solemnly winked his eye.

"What became of the sailor?" asked Dan.

"That sailor was me," admitted the Captain. "That is what became of him. Served him right, too."

Element Focus: Language Usage

What is the surprising end to the descriptive story that the captain shared?

#50986—Leveled Texts for Classic Fiction: Historical Fiction   © Shell Education

The Puritan Twins

by Lucy Fitch Perkins

Daniel was standing on the deck of the Lucy Ann. He was drinking in the fresh salt breeze. He was watching the shores as the boat passed between Charlestown and Boston. It dropped anchor in the harbor to set the Captain's lobster-pots. All day they sailed past rocky islands and picturesque headlands. The Captain was at the tiller skillfully keeping the vessel to the course. At the same time, he was spinning yarns to Daniel and his father about the adventures which had overtaken him at various points along the coast. At Governor's Island, he had caught a giant lobster. He had been all but wrecked in a fog off Thompson's Island.

"Ye see that point of land," he said. He was waving his hand. He pointed toward a rocky promontory extending far out into the bay. "That's Squantum. Miles Standish of Plymouth named it that after an Indian that was a good friend of the Colony in the early days. Right off there I was overhauled by a French privateer once. 'Privateer' is a polite name for a pirate ship. She was loaded with molasses, indigo, and such from the West Indies. I had a cargo of beaver-skins. Her sailors was mostly roarin' drunk at the time. Or else it would have been the end of Thomas Sanders, skipper, sloop, and all. But my boat was smaller and quicker than theirs. I know these waters so well. I was able to give them the slip. I got out into open sea. Here I be! Ah, those were the days!"

The Captain heaved a heavy sigh for the lost joys of youth. He was silent for a moment. Then his eyes twinkled and he began another story. "One day, as we was skirtin' the shores of Martha's Vineyard," he said, "we were followed by a shark. Now, there is nothing a sailor hates worse than a shark. For good reasons. They are the pirates of the deep. That is what they are. They will follow a vessel for days. They snap up whatever the cook throws out. They are hoping somebody will fall overboard to give 'em a full meal. Well, sir, there was a sailor aboard on that voyage that had a special grudge against sharks. He had been all but et up by one once. He allowed this was his chance to get even. So he let out a hook baited with a whole pound of salt pork. The shark gobbled it down instanter, hook and all. They hauled him up the ship's side. Then that sailor let himself down over the rails by a rope. He cut a hole in the shark's gullet, or whatever they call the pouch the critter carries his supplies in. He took out the pork. Then he dropped him back in the water. He threw the pork in after him. Well, sir, believe it or not, that shark sighted the pork bobbing 'round in the water. He swallowed it again. Of course it dropped right out through the hole in his gullet. And, by jolly! As long as we could see him, that shark was continuing to swallow that piece of pork over and over again. I do not know as I ever seen any animal get more pleasure out of his rations than that shark got out of that pound of pork. I believe in bein' kind to dumb critters," he finished. "I reckon the shark is about the dumbdest there is. Anyhow that one surely did die happy." Here the Captain solemnly winked his eye.

"What became of the sailor?" asked Dan.

"That sailor was me," admitted the Captain. "That is what became of him. Served him right, too."

Element Focus: Language Usage

What pictures do the Captain's words paint in your mind?

#50986—Leveled Texts for Classic Fiction: Historical Fiction

The Puritan Twins

by Lucy Fitch Perkins

Meanwhile, Daniel was standing on the deck of the Lucy Ann. He was drinking in the fresh salt breeze. He was eagerly watching the shores as the boat passed between Charlestown and Boston. It dropped anchor in the harbor to set the Captain's lobster-pots. All the wonderful bright day, they sailed past rocky islands and picturesque headlands. The Captain was at the tiller skillfully keeping the vessel to the course, and at the same time spinning yarns to Daniel and his father about the adventures which had overtaken him at various points along the coast. At Governor's Island, he had caught a giant lobster. He had been all but wrecked in a fog off Thompson's Island.

"Ye see that point of land," he said. He was waving his hand toward a rocky promontory extending far out into the bay. "That's Squantum. Miles Standish of Plymouth named it that after an Indian that was a good friend of the Colony in the early days. Well, right off there I was overhauled by a French privateer once. 'Privateer' is a polite name for a pirate ship. She was loaded with molasses, indigo, and such from the West Indies. I had a cargo of beaver-skins. If it hadn't been that her sailors was mostly roarin' drunk at the time, it is likely that would have been the end of Thomas Sanders, skipper, sloop, and all. But my boat was smaller and quicker than theirs. Knowing these waters so well, I was able to give 'em the slip and get out into open sea. Here I be! Ah, those were the days!"

The Captain heaved a heavy sigh for the lost joys of youth. He was silent for a moment. Then his eyes twinkled and he began another story. "One day as we was skirtin' the shores of Martha's Vineyard," he said, "we were followed by a shark. Now, there is nothing a sailor hates worse than a shark; and for good reasons. They're the pirates of the deep; that's what they are. They'll follow a vessel for days, snapping up whatever the cook throws out, and hoping somebody'll fall overboard to give 'em a full meal. Well, sir, there was a sailor aboard on that voyage that had a special grudge against sharks. He'd been all but et up by one once, and he allowed this was his chance to get even; so he let out a hook baited with a whole pound of salt pork, and the shark gobbled it down instanter, hook and all. They hauled him up the ship's side, and then that sailor let himself down over the rails by a rope, and cut a hole in the shark's gullet, or whatever they call the pouch the critter carries his supplies in, and took out the pork. Then he dropped him back in the water and threw the pork in after him. Well, sir, believe it or not, that shark sighted the pork bobbing round in the water; so he swallowed it again. Of course it dropped right out through the hole in his gullet, and, by jolly, as long as we could see him that shark was continuing to swallow that piece of pork over and over again. I don't know as I ever seen any animal get more pleasure out of his rations than that shark got out of that pound of pork. I believe in bein' kind to dumb critters," he finished, "and I reckon the shark is about the dumbdest there is. Anyhow that one surely did die happy." Here the Captain solemnly winked his eye.

"What became of the sailor?" asked Dan.

"That sailor was me," admitted the Captain. "That's what became of him, and served him right, too."

Element Focus: Language Usage

What descriptive words does the captain use to describe sharks? What other words would you use?

#50986—Leveled Texts for Classic Fiction: Historical Fiction

The Puritan Twins

by Lucy Fitch Perkins

Meanwhile Daniel was standing on the deck of the Lucy Ann, drinking in the fresh salt breeze and eagerly watching the shores as the boat passed between Charlestown and Boston and dropped anchor in the harbor to set the Captain's lobster-pots. All the wonderful bright day they sailed past rocky islands and picturesque headlands, with the Captain at the tiller skillfully keeping the vessel to the course and at the same time spinning yarns to Daniel and his father about the adventures which had overtaken him at various points along the coast. At Governor's Island he had caught a giant lobster. He had been all but wrecked in a fog off Thompson's Island.

"Ye see that point of land," he said, waving his hand toward a rocky promontory extending far out into the bay. "That's Squantum. Miles Standish of Plymouth named it that after an Indian that was a good friend of the Colony in the early days. Well, right off there I was overhauled by a French privateer once. 'Privateer' is a polite name for a pirate ship. She was loaded with molasses, indigo, and such from the West Indies, and I had a cargo of beaver-skins. If it hadn't been that her sailors was mostly roarin' drunk at the time, it's likely that would have been the end of Thomas Sanders, skipper, sloop, and all, but my boat was smaller and quicker than theirs, and, knowing these waters so well, I was able to give 'em the slip and get out into open sea; and here I be! Ah, those were the days!"

The Captain heaved a heavy sigh for the lost joys of youth and was silent for a moment. Then his eyes twinkled and he began another story. "One day as we was skirtin' the shores of Martha's Vineyard," he said, "we were followed by a shark. Now, there's nothing a sailor hates worse than a shark; and for good reasons. They're the pirates of the deep; that's what they are. They'll follow a vessel for days, snapping up whatever the cook throws out, and hoping somebody'll fall overboard to give 'em a full meal. Well, sir, there was a sailor aboard on that voyage that had a special grudge against sharks. He'd been all but et up by one once, and he allowed this was his chance to get even; so he let out a hook baited with a whole pound of salt pork, and the shark gobbled it down instanter, hook and all. They hauled him up the ship's side, and then that sailor let himself down over the rails by a rope, and cut a hole in the shark's gullet, or whatever they call the pouch the critter carries his supplies in, and took out the pork. Then he dropped him back in the water and threw the pork in after him. Well, sir, believe it or not, that shark sighted the pork bobbing round in the water; so he swallowed it again. Of course it dropped right out through the hole in his gullet, and, by jolly! As long as we could see him that shark was continuing to swallow that piece of pork over and over again. I don't know as I ever see any animal get more pleasure out of his rations than that shark got out of that pound of pork. I believe in bein' kind to dumb critters," he finished, "and I reckon the shark is about the dumbdest there is. Anyhow that one surely did die happy." Here the Captain solemnly winked his eye.

"What became of the sailor?" asked Dan.

"That sailor was me," admitted the Captain. "That's what became of him, and served him right, too."

Element Focus: Language Usage

What examples from the language of this story tell the reader that a sailor tells the tale?

#50986—*Leveled Texts for Classic Fiction: Historical Fiction*   © *Shell Education*

The Red Badge of Courage

by Stephen Crane

A fat soldier tried to steal a horse. He planned to load his backpack upon it. He was escaping with his prize. A young girl rushed from the house. She grabbed the animal's mane. There followed a wrangle. The young girl had pink cheeks. She had shining eyes. She stood like a statue.

The regiment was observant. The soldiers were in the roadway. They whooped at once. They were on the side of the girl. The men became engrossed in this affair. They entirely ceased to remember their own large war. They jeered the piratical private. They called attention to various defects in his personal appearance. They were wildly enthusiastic in support of the young girl.

Someone spoke to her. The words came from some distance. It was bold advice. "Hit him with a stick!"

There were crows. There were catcalls. They were showered upon him. He retreated without the horse. The regiment rejoiced at his downfall. Loud congratulations were showered upon the girl. She stood panting. She regarded the troops with defiance.

It was nightfall. The column broke into regimental pieces. The fragments camped the fields. Tents sprang up like strange plants. Campfires were like red, strange blossoms. They dotted the night.

The youth stayed away from his companions. In the evening, he wandered a few paces into the gloom. He saw the many fires. There were black forms of men passing to and fro before the crimson rays. The forms made weird effects.

The boy lay down in the grass. The blades pressed kindly against his cheek. The moon had been lighted. It was hung in a treetop. The night was a liquid stillness. It made him feel vast pity for himself. There was a caress in the soft winds. The whole mood of the darkness was one of sympathy for himself in his distress.

He wished that he was at home. He wanted to make endless rounds. He would go from the house to the barn to the field and back. He had often cursed the brindle cow. He also cursed her mates. He had sometimes flung milking stools. Now there was a halo of happiness about each of their heads. He would have sacrificed a lot to be able to return to them. He told himself that he was not formed for a soldier. He thought about his differences. He was not like the men who were dodging implike around the fires.

He heard the rustle of grass. He turned his head. He discovered the loud soldier. He called out, "Oh, Wilson!"

The latter approached. He looked down. "Why, hello Henry. Is it you? What you doing here?"

"Oh, thinking," said the youth.

The other sat down. He lighted his pipe. He did this carefully. "You are getting blue, my boy. What the dickens is wrong with you?"

"Oh, nothing," said the youth.

The loud soldier launched into the subject of the coming fight. "Oh, we have got them now!" He had a boyish face. It showed a gleeful smile. His voice had an exultant ring. "We have got them now. We will lick them good!"

"The truth may be known," he added. This time he said it more soberly. "They have licked US about every clip up to now. This time we will lick them good!"

Element Focus: Language Usage

What is the setting that is detailed using descriptive language?

#50986—Leveled Texts for Classic Fiction: Historical Fiction

Excerpt from

The Red Badge of Courage

by Stephen Crane

A rather fat soldier attempted to pilfer a horse from a dooryard. He planned to load his backpack upon it. He was escaping with his prize. A young girl rushed from the house. She grabbed the animal's mane. There followed a wrangle. The young girl had pink cheeks and shining eyes. She stood like a bold statue.

The observant regiment was standing at rest in the roadway. They whooped at once. They entered whole-souled upon the side of the maiden. The men became very engrossed in this affair. They entirely ceased to remember their own large war. They jeered the piratical private. They called attention to various defects in his personal appearance. They were wildly excited in support of the young girl.

To her, from some distance, came bold advice. "Hit him with a stick!"

There were crows and catcalls showered upon him when he retreated without the horse. The regiment cheered at his downfall. Loud and vociferous congratulations were showered upon the girl. She stood panting and regarding the troops with defiance.

At nightfall, the column broke into regimental pieces. The fragments went into the fields to camp. Tents sprang up like strange plants. Campfires, like red, strange blossoms, dotted the night.

The youth kept from contact with his companions as much as circumstances would allow him. In the evening, he wandered a few paces into the gloom. From this little distance, he saw the many fires. The black forms of men passing to and fro before the crimson rays made weird and satanic effects.

He lay down in the grass. The blades pressed tenderly against his cheek. The moon had been lighted. It was hung in a treetop. The liquid stillness of the night enveloping him made him feel vast pity for himself. There was a caress in the soft winds. The whole mood of the darkness, he thought, was one of sympathy for himself in his distress.

He wished, without reserve, that he was at home again. He wanted to make the endless rounds from the house to the barn. Then he would go from the barn to the fields. Then from the fields to the barn. Finally, he would go from the barn to the house. He remembered he had often cursed the brindle cow and her mates. He had sometimes flung milking stools. But, from his present point of view, there was a halo of happiness about each of their heads. He would have sacrificed all the brass buttons on the continent to have been enabled to return to them. He told himself that he was not formed for a soldier. He mused seriously upon the radical differences between himself and those men who were dodging implike around the fires.

As he mused thus, he heard the rustle of grass. Upon turning his head, he discovered the loud soldier. He called out, "Oh, Wilson!"

The latter approached and looked down. "Why, hello Henry. Is it you? What you doing here?"

"Oh, thinking," said the youth.

The other sat down. He carefully lighted his pipe. "You are getting blue, my boy. You are looking thundering peek-ed. What the dickens is wrong with you?"

"Oh, nothing," said the youth.

The loud soldier launched then into the subject of the expected fight. "Oh, we've got 'em now!" As he spoke, his boyish face was wreathed in a thrilled smile. His voice had a happy ring. "We have got 'em now. At last, by the eternal thunders, we'll lick 'em good!"

"If the truth was known," he added, more soberly, "they've licked US about every clip up to now. This time we will lick 'em good!"

Element Focus: Language Usage

What do you visualize when you read about Henry lying down in the grass?

#50986—Leveled Texts for Classic Fiction: Historical Fiction

The Red Badge of Courage

by Stephen Crane

A rather fat soldier tried to steal a horse from a dooryard. He planned to load his knapsack upon it. He was escaping with his prize when a young girl rushed from the house and grabbed the animal's mane. There followed a wrangle. The young girl, with pink cheeks and shining eyes, stood like a dauntless statue.

The observant regiment, standing at rest in the roadway, whooped at once, and entered whole-souled upon the side of the maiden. The men became so engrossed in this affair that they fully ceased to remember their own large war. They jeered the piratical private, and called attention to various defects in his personal appearance; and they were wildly enthusiastic in support of the young girl.

To her, from some distance, came bold advice. "Hit him with a stick."

There were crows and catcalls showered upon him when he retreated without the horse. The regiment rejoiced at his downfall. Loud and vociferous congratulations were showered upon the maiden, who stood panting and regarding the troops with defiance.

At nightfall, the column broke into regimental pieces, and the fragments went into the fields to camp. Tents sprang up like strange plants. Campfires, like red, peculiar blossoms, dotted the night.

The youth kept from contact with his companions as much as circumstances would allow him. In the evening, he wandered a few paces into the gloom. From this little distance, the many fires with the black forms of men passing to and fro before the crimson rays made weird and satanic effects.

He lay down in the grass. The blades pressed kindly against his cheek. The moon had been lighted and was hung in a treetop. The liquid stillness of the night enveloping him made him feel vast pity for himself. There was a caress in the soft winds; and the whole mood of the darkness, he thought, was one of sympathy for himself in his distress.

He wished, without reserve, that he was at home again making the endless rounds from the house to the barn, from the barn to the fields, from the fields to the barn, from the barn to the house. He remembered he had often cursed the brindle cow and her mates, and had sometimes flung milking stools. But, from his present point of view, there was a halo of happiness about each of their heads, and he would have sacrificed all the brass buttons on the continent to have been enabled to return to them. He told himself that he was not formed for a soldier. And he mused seriously upon the radical differences between himself and those men who were dodging implike around the fires.

As he mused thus he heard the rustle of grass, and, upon turning his head, discovered the loud soldier. He called out, "Oh, Wilson!"

The latter approached and looked down. "Why, hello, Henry; is it you? What you doing here?"

"Oh, thinking," said the youth.

The other sat down and carefully lighted his pipe. "You're getting blue my boy. You're looking thundering peek-ed. What the dickens is wrong with you?"

"Oh, nothing," said the youth.

The loud soldier launched then into the subject of the anticipated fight. "Oh, we've got 'em now!" As he spoke his boyish face was wreathed in a gleeful smile, and his voice had an exultant ring. "We've got 'em now. At last, by the eternal thunders, we'll lick 'em good!"

"If the truth was known," he added, more soberly, "they've licked US about every clip up to now; but this time—this time—we'll lick 'em good!"

Element Focus: Language Usage

What words does the author use to describe the tents and campfires, and what does this description make you visualize as you read?

#50986—Leveled Texts for Classic Fiction: Historical Fiction

Excerpt from

The Red Badge of Courage

by Stephen Crane

A rather fat soldier attempted to pilfer a horse from a dooryard as he planned to load his knapsack upon it. He was escaping with his prize when a young girl rushed from the house and grabbed the animal's mane, and there followed a wrangle. The young girl, with pink cheeks and shining eyes, stood like a dauntless statue.

The observant regiment, standing at rest in the roadway, whooped at once, and entered whole-souled upon the side of the maiden. The men became so engrossed in this affair that they entirely ceased to remember their own large war while they jeered the piratical private, and called attention to various defects in his personal appearance; and they were wildly enthusiastic in support of the young girl.

To her, from some distance, came bold advice. "Hit him with a stick!"

There were crows and catcalls showered upon him when he retreated without the horse as the regiment rejoiced at his downfall. Loud and vociferous congratulations were showered upon the maiden, who stood panting and regarding the troops with defiance.

At nightfall, the column broke into regimental pieces, and the fragments went into the fields to camp. Tents sprang up like strange plants. Campfires, like red, peculiar blossoms, dotted the night.

The youth kept from contact with his companions as much as circumstances would allow him. In the evening, he wandered a few paces into the gloom. From this little distance, the many fires with the black forms of men passing to and fro before the crimson rays made weird and satanic effects.

He lay down in the grass while the blades pressed tenderly against his cheek. The moon had been lighted and was hung in a treetop. The liquid stillness of the night enveloping him made him feel vast pity for himself. There was a caress in the soft winds; and the whole mood of the darkness, he thought, was one of sympathy for himself in his distress.

He wished, without reserve, that he was at home again making the endless rounds from the house to the barn, from the barn to the fields, from the fields to the barn, from the barn to the house. He remembered he had often cursed the brindle cow and her mates, and had sometimes flung milking stools—but, from his present point of view, there was a halo of happiness about each of their heads, and he would have sacrificed all the brass buttons on the continent to have been enabled to return to them. He told himself that he was not formed for a soldier, and he mused seriously upon the radical differences between himself and those men who were dodging implike around the fires.

As he mused thus, he heard the rustle of grass, and, upon turning his head, discovered the loud soldier as he called out, "Oh, Wilson!"

The latter approached and looked down. "Why, hello, Henry; is it you? What you doing here?"

"Oh, thinking," said the youth.

The other sat down and carefully lighted his pipe. "You're getting blue, my boy; you're looking thundering peek-ed. What the dickens is wrong with you?"

"Oh, nothing," said the youth.

The loud soldier launched then into the subject of the anticipated fight. "Oh, we've got 'em now!" As he spoke, his boyish face was wreathed in a gleeful smile, and his voice had an exultant ring. "We've got 'em now, at last, by the eternal thunders, we'll lick 'em good!"

"If the truth was known," he added, more soberly, "they've licked US about every clip up to now; but this time—this time—we'll lick 'em good!"

Element Focus: Language Usage

What examples of simile and metaphor can you find in this story? Why do you think the author used this style of writing?

#50986—Leveled Texts for Classic Fiction: Historical Fiction

Excerpt from

The Secret Garden

by Frances Hodgson Burnett

Mary asked no more questions. She waited in the darkness. She kept her eyes on the window. The carriage lamps cast rays of light a little distance ahead of them. She caught glimpses of the things they passed. They had left the station. They had driven through a tiny village. She had seen whitewashed cottages. She saw the lights of a public house. Then they had passed a church. They also passed a vicarage. They passed a little shop window or so in a cottage. It had toys and sweets. There were odd things set out for sale. Then they were on the high road. She saw hedges and trees. After that, there seemed nothing different for a long time. At least, it seemed a long time to her.

The horses began to go more slowly. It was as if they were climbing uphill. There seemed to be no more hedges and no more trees. She could see nothing but a dense darkness on either side. She leaned forward. She pressed her face against the window. The carriage gave a big jolt.

"We are on the moor now sure enough," said Mrs. Medlock.

The carriage lamps shed a yellow light. There was a rough-looking road. It seemed to be cut through bushes and low-growing things. It ended in the great expanse of dark. The dark was apparently spread out. It was before and around them. A wind was rising. It was making a singular sound. It was wild and low.

"It is not the sea, is it?" said Mary. She looked at her companion.

"No. It is not it," answered Mrs. Medlock. "Nor is it fields nor mountains. It is just miles and miles of wild land. Nothing grows on it but heather and gorse and broom. Nothing lives on it but wild ponies and sheep."

"I feel as if it might be the sea. If there were water on it," said Mary. "It sounds like the sea just now."

"That is the wind blowing through the bushes," Mrs. Medlock said. "It is a wild, dreary enough place to my mind. Though there is plenty that likes it. Particularly when the heather is in bloom."

On and on they drove through the darkness. The rain stopped. The wind rushed by. It whistled and made strange sounds. The road went up and down. Several times the carriage passed over a little bridge. Beneath it the water rushed very fast. It made a great deal of noise. Mary felt as if the drive would never come to an end. She thought the wide, bleak moor was a wide expanse of black ocean through which she was passing on a strip of dry land.

"I do not like it," she said to herself. "I do not like it." She pinched her thin lips more tightly together.

The horses were climbing up a hilly piece of road. Then she first caught sight of a light. Mrs. Medlock saw it as soon as she did. She drew a long sigh of relief.

"I am glad to see that bit o' light twinkling," she exclaimed. "It is the light in the lodge window. We shall get a good cup of tea after a bit, at all events."

It was "after a bit," as she said. The carriage passed through the park gates. There was still two miles of avenue to drive through. The trees (which nearly met overhead) made it seem as if they were driving through a long, dark vault.

They drove out of the vault. They went into a clear space and stopped. They were before an immensely long but low-built house. The house seemed to ramble is 'round a stone court. At first, Mary thought that there were no lights at all in the windows. As she got out of the carriage, she saw that one room in a corner upstairs showed a dull glow.

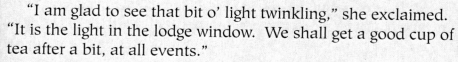

Element Focus: Language Usage

How does the author describe the moor?

Excerpt from

The Secret Garden

by Frances Hodgson Burnett

Mary asked no more questions. She waited in the darkness of her corner. She kept her eyes on the window. The carriage lamps cast rays of light a little distance ahead of them. She caught glimpses of the things they passed. They had left the station and driven through a tiny village. She had seen whitewashed cottages. She saw the lights of a public house. Then they had passed a church and a vicarage. They passed a little shop window or so in a cottage. It had toys and sweets and odd things set out for sale. Then they were on the high road. She saw hedges and trees. After that, there seemed nothing different for a long time. At least it seemed a long time to her.

At last, the horses began to go more slowly. It was as if they were climbing uphill. Presently, there seemed to be no more hedges and no more trees. She could see nothing but a dense darkness on either side. She leaned forward. She pressed her face against the window. The carriage gave a big jolt.

"Eh! We are on the moor now sure enough," said Mrs. Medlock.

The carriage lamps shed a yellow light on a rough-looking road. It seemed to be cut through bushes and low-growing things. It ended in the great expanse of dark apparently spread out before and around them. A wind was rising. It was making a singular, wild, low, rushing sound.

"It is not the sea, is it?" said Mary. She looked round at her companion.

"No, not it," answered Mrs. Medlock. "Nor it isn't fields nor mountains. It is just miles and miles and miles of wild land. Nothing grows on it but heather and gorse and broom. Nothing lives on it but wild ponies and sheep."

"I feel as if it might be the sea. If there were water on it," said Mary. "It sounds like the sea just now."

"That is the wind blowing through the bushes," Mrs. Medlock said. "It is a wild, dreary enough place to my mind, though there's plenty that likes it—particularly when the heather's in bloom."

On and on they drove through the darkness. Though the rain stopped, the wind rushed by and whistled and made strange sounds. The road went up and down, and several times the carriage passed over a little bridge beneath which water rushed very fast with a great deal of noise. Mary felt as if the drive would never come to an end and that the wide, bleak moor was a wide expanse of black ocean through which she was passing on a strip of dry land.

"I don't like it," she said to herself. "I don't like it." She pinched her thin lips more tightly together.

The horses were climbing up a hilly piece of road when she first caught sight of a light. Mrs. Medlock saw it as soon as she did and drew a long sigh of relief.

"Eh, I am glad to see that bit o' light twinkling," she exclaimed. "It's the light in the lodge window. We shall get a good cup of tea after a bit, at all events."

It was "after a bit," as she said, for when the carriage passed through the park gates, there was still two miles of avenue to drive through and the trees (which nearly met overhead) made it seem as if they were driving through a long, dark vault.

They drove out of the vault into a clear space and stopped before an immensely long but low-built house which seemed to ramble 'round a stone court. At first, Mary thought that there were no lights at all in the windows, but as she got out of the carriage, she saw that one room in a corner upstairs showed a dull glow.

Element Focus: Language Usage

Which descriptive words help you imagine the journey that Mary is taking? What are some images you can picture?

#50986—Leveled Texts for Classic Fiction: Historical Fiction

Excerpt from

The Secret Garden

by Frances Hodgson Burnett

Mary asked no more questions. She waited in the darkness of her corner, keeping her eyes on the window. The carriage lamps cast rays of light a little distance ahead of them. She caught glimpses of the things they passed. After they had left the station, they had driven through a tiny village. She had seen whitewashed cottages and the lights of a public house. Then they had passed a church and a vicarage and a little shop window or so in a cottage with toys and sweets and odd things set out for sale. Then they were on the high road. She saw hedges and trees. After that, there seemed nothing different for a long time—at least, it seemed a long time to her.

At last, the horses began to go more slowly, as if they were climbing uphill. Presently, there seemed to be no more hedges and no more trees. She could see nothing, in fact, but a dense darkness on either side. She leaned forward and pressed her face against the window just as the carriage gave an immense jolt.

"Eh! We're on the moor now sure enough," said Mrs. Medlock.

The carriage lamps shed a yellow light on a rough-looking road. It seemed to be cut through bushes and low-growing things which ended in the great expanse of dark apparently spread out before and around them. A wind was rising and making a singular, wild, low, rushing sound.

"It's—it's not the sea, is it?" said Mary, looking round at her companion.

"No, not it," answered Mrs. Medlock. "Nor it isn't fields nor mountains; it's just miles and miles and miles of wild land that nothing grows on but heather and gorse and broom. Nothing lives on it but wild ponies and sheep."

"I feel as if it might be the sea, if there were water on it," said Mary. "It sounds like the sea just now."

"That's the wind blowing through the bushes," Mrs. Medlock said. "It's a wild, dreary enough place to my mind, though there's plenty that likes it—particularly when the heather's in bloom."

On and on they drove through the darkness. Though the rain stopped, the wind hurried by and whistled and made bizarre sounds. The road went up and down, and several times the carriage passed over a little bridge beneath which water rushed very fast with a great deal of noise. Mary felt as if the drive would never come to an end and that the wide, bleak moor was a wide expanse of black ocean through which she was passing on a strip of dry land.

"I don't like it," she said to herself. "I don't like it." She pinched her thin lips more tightly together.

The horses were climbing up a hilly piece of road when she first caught sight of a light. Mrs. Medlock saw it as soon as she did and drew a long sigh of relief.

"Eh, I am glad to see that bit o' light twinkling," she exclaimed. "It's the light in the lodge window. We shall get a good cup of tea after a bit, at all events."

It was "after a bit," as she said, for when the carriage passed through the park gates, there was still two miles of avenue to drive through and the trees (which nearly met overhead) made it seem as if they were driving through a long, dark vault.

They drove out of the vault into a clear area and stopped before an immensely long but low-built house which seemed to ramble 'round a stone court. At first, Mary thought that there were no lights at all in the windows, but as she got out of the carriage, she saw that one room in a corner upstairs showed a gloomy glow.

Element Focus: Language Usage

How can you improve upon the word selection for this passage?

#50986—Leveled Texts for Classic Fiction: Historical Fiction   © Shell Education

Excerpt from

The Secret Garden

by Frances Hodgson Burnett

Mary asked no more questions but waited in the darkness of her corner, keeping her eyes on the window. The carriage lamps cast rays of light a little distance ahead of them and she caught glimpses of the things they passed. After they had left the station, they had driven through a tiny village and she had seen whitewashed cottages and the lights of a public house. Then they had passed a church and a vicarage and a little shop-window or so in a cottage with toys and sweets and odd things set out for sale. Then they were on the highroad and she saw hedges and trees. After that there seemed nothing different for a long time— or at least it seemed a long time to her.

At last the horses began to go more slowly, as if they were climbing uphill, and presently there seemed to be no more hedges and no more trees. She could see nothing, in fact, but a dense darkness on either side. She leaned forward and pressed her face against the window just as the carriage gave a big jolt.

"Eh! We're on the moor now sure enough," said Mrs. Medlock.

The carriage lamps shed a yellow light on a rough-looking road which seemed to be cut through bushes and low-growing things that ended in the great expanse of dark apparently spread out before and around them. A wind was rising and making a singular, wild, low, rushing sound.

"It's—it's not the sea, is it?" said Mary, looking round at her companion.

"No, not it," answered Mrs. Medlock. "Nor it isn't fields nor mountains; it's just miles and miles and miles of wild land that nothing grows on but heather and gorse and broom, and nothing lives on but wild ponies and sheep."

"I feel as if it might be the sea, if there were water on it," said Mary. "It sounds like the sea just now."

"That's the wind blowing through the bushes," Mrs. Medlock said. "It's a wild, dreary enough place to my mind, though there's plenty that likes it—particularly when the heather's in bloom."

On and on they drove through the darkness, and though the rain stopped, the wind rushed by and whistled and made strange sounds. The road went up and down, and several times the carriage passed over a little bridge beneath which water rushed very fast with a great deal of noise. Mary felt as if the drive would never come to an end and that the wide, bleak moor was a wide expanse of black ocean through which she was passing on a strip of dry land.

"I don't like it," she said to herself. "I don't like it," and she pinched her thin lips more tightly together.

The horses were climbing up a hilly piece of road when she first caught sight of a light. Mrs. Medlock saw it as soon as she did and drew a long sigh of relief.

"Eh, I am glad to see that bit o' light twinkling," she exclaimed. "It's the light in the lodge window. We shall get a good cup of tea after a bit, at all events."

It was "after a bit," as she said, for when the carriage passed through the park gates there was still two miles of avenue to drive through and the trees (which nearly met overhead) made it seem as if they were driving through a long dark vault.

They drove out of the vault into a clear space and stopped before an immensely long but low-built house which seemed to ramble round a stone court. At first Mary thought that there were no lights at all in the windows, but as she got out of the carriage, she saw that one room in a corner upstairs showed a dull glow.

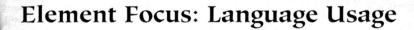

Element Focus: Language Usage

Describe how the author uses sensory language.

Excerpt from

The Guns of Bull Run

by Joseph A. Altsheler

Harry did fall asleep after a while. He awoke before dawn. There was already movement. It was in the army about him. Fires were lighted farther back. An early breakfast was cooked. The food was plentiful. All were up and ready. The sun rose. It moved over the Virginia fields.

"Another hot day," said Happy Tom. "The sun is as red as fire! And look how it burns on the water there."

"Hot it will be," Harry said. He talked to himself. They had eaten their breakfast. Now they lay once more among the trees. Harry searched with his eyes. He saw bushes and thickets on the other side. He looked for their riflemen. Most of them were still invisible in the day. Then the Southern brigades were ordered to lie down. They lay there some time. Harry felt the film of dust on the edge of the wind was growing stronger. They saw a great cloud of it. It was rising above hills and trees. It was moving toward them.

"They are coming," said St. Clair. "They will be at the ford. It will be in less than a half hour."

"I doubt if they know what is waiting for them," said Harry.

The cloud of dust came nearer. It moved rapidly. They heard the beat of horses' feet. They heard the clank of artillery. Harry began to breathe hard. He and the other young officers walked up and down. They moved in their company lines. All the Invincibles clearly saw it. It was a great plume of dust. They heard ominous sounds, too. It was very near now. Suddenly, the fringe of forest burst into flame. It was on the far side of the river. The hidden riflemen opened fire. They were burning the front of the advancing army.

The Northern men came steadily on. They were rousing the riflemen out of the bushes. Then they appeared. They were among the trees. It was on the north side of Bull Run. It was a New York brigade. They were led by Tyler. Their faces showed. There was a tremendous discharge of sound. It came from the Southern batteries. They had been hidden in the wood. The crash was appalling. Harry shut his eyes for a moment. He did it to shut out the horror. He saw the entire front rank of the Northern force go down. Then the Southern sharpshooters opened with their rifles. There were hundreds who lined the water's edge. A storm of lead crashed. It went right into the ranks of the hapless New Yorkers.

"Get up!" cried Colonel Talbot. They began to fire. They loaded. They fired again into the attacking force. The force had walked into an ambush.

"They will never reach the ford!" shouted Happy Tom.

"Never!" Harry shouted back.

The Southern generals were already trained in battle. They pushed their advantages. A great force of Southern sharpshooters crossed the river. They took the Northern brigade on the flank. The New Yorkers could not stand the artillery and rifle fire in their front. They broke. They retreated. There was new rifle fire on their side, also. Another brigade came up to their relief. They advanced again. They sent a heavy return fire from their rifles. The artillery on their flank replied to that of the South.

The combat became fierce. There were Invincibles in the very thick of it. They advanced to the water's edge. They fired as fast as they could. It took time to load and reload. Huge volumes of smoke gathered. It moved over both sides of Bull Run. Men fell fast. Twigs and boughs rained down. The bullets and shells cut them through. The air was dense and heated. It was a shot through with smoke. It burned the throats of blue and gray.

Element Focus: Language Usage

How do the words set the mood or tone?

Excerpt from

The Guns of Bull Run

by Joseph A. Altsheler

Harry did fall asleep after a while. He awoke before dawn. He found that there was already bustle and movement in the army about him. Fires were lighted farther back. An early but plentiful breakfast was cooked. All were up and ready. The sun rose over the Virginia fields.

"Another hot day," said Happy Tom. "The sun is as red as fire! And look how it burns on the water there."

"Hot it will be," Harry said to himself. They had eaten their breakfast. Now they lay once more among the trees. Harry searched with his eyes the bushes and thickets on the other side. He looked for their riflemen. Most of them were still invisible in the day. Then the Southern brigades were ordered to lie down. They lay there some time. Then Harry felt that the film of dust on the edge of the wind was growing stronger. They saw a great cloud of it rising above hills and trees. It was moving toward them.

"They are coming," said St. Clair. "In less than a half hour, they will be at the ford."

"But I doubt if they know what is waiting for them," said Harry.

The cloud of dust rapidly came nearer. Now they heard the beat of horses' feet. They heard the clank of artillery. Harry began to breathe hard. He and the other young officers walked up and down the lines of their company. All the Invincibles clearly saw that great plume of dust. They heard the ominous sounds that came with it. It was very near now. Suddenly, the fringe of forest on the far side of the river burst into flame. The hidden riflemen had opened fire. They were burning the front of the advancing army.

But the Northern men came steadily on. They were rousing the riflemen out of the bushes. Then they appeared among the trees on the north side of Bull Run. It was a New York brigade led by Tyler. The moment their faces showed, there was a tremendous discharge from the Southern batteries masked in the wood. The crash was appalling. Harry shut his eyes for a moment. He did it to shut out the horror. He saw the entire front rank of the Northern force go down. Then the Southern sharpshooters opened with their rifles. There were hundreds who lined the water's edge. A storm of lead crashed into the ranks of the hapless New Yorkers.

"Up, Invincibles!" cried Colonel Talbot. They began to fire. They loaded. They fired again into the attacking force. The force had walked into what was almost an ambush.

"They will never reach the ford!" shouted Happy Tom.

"Never!" Harry shouted back.

The Southern generals were already trained in battle. They pushed their advantages. A great force of Southern sharpshooters crossed the river. They took the Northern brigade on the flank. The New Yorkers were unable to stand the tremendous artillery and rifle fire in their front. They broke and retreated. There was new rifle fire on their side, also. But another brigade came up to their relief. They advanced again. They sent a heavy return fire from their rifles. The artillery on their flank replied to that of the South.

The combat now became fierce. The Invincibles in the very thick of it advanced to the water's edge, and fired as fast as they could load and reload. Huge volumes of smoke gathered over both sides of Bull Run, and men fell fast. There was also a rain of twigs and boughs as the bullets and shells cut them through, and the dense, heated air, shot through with smoke, burned the throats of blue and gray.

Element Focus: Language Usage

What is a better way of describing this passage? Why?

#50986—Leveled Texts for Classic Fiction: Historical Fiction

Excerpt from

The Guns of Bull Run

by Joseph A. Altsheler

Harry did fall asleep after a while. He awoke before dawn to find that there was already bustle and movement in the army about him. Fires were lighted farther back. An early but plentiful breakfast was cooked. All were up and ready when the sun rose over the Virginia fields.

"Another hot day," said Happy Tom. "See, the sun is as red as fire! And look how it burns on the water there."

"Yes, hot it will be," Harry said to himself. They had eaten their breakfast and lay once more among the trees. Harry searched with his eyes the bushes and thickets on the other side for their riflemen. Most of them were still invisible in the day. Then the Southern brigades were ordered to lie down. After they lay there some time, Harry felt that the film of dust on the edge of the wind was growing stronger. They saw a great cloud of it rising above hills and trees and moving toward them.

"They are coming," said St. Clair. "In less than a half hour, they'll be at the ford."

"But I doubt if they know what is waiting for them," said Harry.

The cloud of dust rapidly came nearer. Now they heard the beat of horses' feet and the clank of artillery. Harry began to breathe hard. He and the other young officers walked up and down the lines of their company. All the Invincibles clearly saw that great plume of dust. They heard the ominous sounds that came with it. It was very near now. Suddenly, the fringe of forest on the far side of the river burst into flame. The hidden riflemen had opened fire and were burning the front of the advancing army.

But the Northern men came steadily on, rousing the riflemen out of the bushes. Then they appeared among the trees on the north side of Bull Run—a New York brigade led by Tyler. The moment their faces showed there was a tremendous discharge from the Southern batteries masked in the wood. The crash was appalling. Harry shut his eyes for a moment in horror. He saw the entire front rank of the Northern force go down. Then the Southern sharpshooters in hundreds, who lined the water's edge, opened with their rifles. A storm of lead crashed into the ranks of the hapless New Yorkers.

"Up, Invincibles!" cried Colonel Talbot. They began to fire, and load, and fire again into the attacking force which had walked into what was almost an ambush.

"They'll never reach the ford!" shouted Happy Tom.

"Never!" Harry shouted back.

The Southern generals, already trained in battle, pushed their advantages. A great force of Southern sharpshooters crossed the river and took the Northern brigade on the flank. The New Yorkers, unable to stand the tremendous artillery and rifle fire in their front and the new rifle fire on their side, also, broke and retreated. But another brigade came up to their relief and they advanced again, sending a heavy return fire from their rifles, while the artillery on their flank replied to that of the South.

The combat now became fierce. The Invincibles in the very thick of it advanced to the water's edge and fired as fast as they could load and reload. Huge volumes of smoke gathered over both sides of Bull Run, and men fell fast. There was also a rain of twigs and boughs as the bullets and shells cut them through, and the dense, heated air, shot through with smoke, burned the throats of blue and gray.

Element Focus: Language Usage

What sounds are described in this story? Why do you think the author used this style of writing?

#50986—Leveled Texts for Classic Fiction: Historical Fiction
© Shell Education

Excerpt from

The Guns of Bull Run

by Joseph A. Altsheler

Harry did fall asleep after a while, but he awoke before dawn to find that there was already bustle and movement in the army about him. Fires were lighted further back, and an early but plentiful breakfast was cooked. All were up and ready when the sun rose over the Virginia fields.

"Another hot day," said Happy Tom. "See, the sun is as red as fire! And look how it burns on the water there."

"Yes, hot it will be," Harry said to himself. They had eaten their breakfast and lay once more among the trees. Harry searched with his eyes the bushes and thickets on the other side for their riflemen, but most of them were still invisible in the day. Then the Southern brigades were ordered to lie down, but after they lay there some time Harry felt that the film of dust on the edge of the wind was growing stronger, and presently they saw a great cloud of it rising above hills and trees and moving toward them.

"They're coming," said St. Clair. "In less than a half hour they'll be at the ford."

"But I doubt if they know what is waiting for them," said Harry.

The cloud of dust rapidly came nearer, and now they heard the beat of horses' feet and the clank of artillery. Harry began to breathe hard, and he and the other young officers walked up and down the lines of their company. All the Invincibles clearly saw that great plume of dust, and heard the ominous sounds that came with it. It was very near now, but suddenly the fringe of forest on the far side of the river burst into flame. The hidden riflemen had opened fire and were burning the front of the advancing army.

But the Northern men came steadily on, rousing the riflemen out of the bushes, and then they appeared among the trees on the north side of Bull Run—a New York brigade led by Tyler. The moment their faces showed there was a tremendous discharge from the Southern batteries masked in the wood. The crash was appalling, and Harry shut his eyes for a moment, in horror, as he saw the entire front rank of the Northern force go down. Then the Southern sharpshooters in hundreds, who lined the water's edge, opened with the rifle, and a storm of lead crashed into the ranks of the hapless New Yorkers.

"Up, Invincibles!" cried Colonel Talbot, and they began to fire, and load, and fire again into the attacking force which had walked into what was almost an ambush.

"They'll never reach the ford!" shouted Happy Tom.

"Never!" Harry shouted back.

The Southern generals, already trained in battles, pushed their advantages. A great force of Southern sharpshooters crossed the river and took the Northern brigade in flank. The New Yorkers, unable to stand the tremendous artillery and rifle fire in their front, and the new rifle fire on their side also, broke and retreated. But another brigade came up to their relief and they advanced again, sending a heavy return fire from their rifles, while the artillery on their flank replied to that of the South.

The combat now became fierce. The Invincibles in the very thick of it advanced to the water's edge, and fired as fast as they could load and reload. Huge volumes of smoke gathered over both sides of Bull Run, and men fell fast. There was also a rain of twigs and boughs as the bullets and shells cut them through, and the dense, heated air, shot through with smoke, burned the throats of blue and gray.

Element Focus: Language Usage

What are some words that helped build anticipation and suspense in the story? Why do you think the author selected these words?

References Cited

Bean, Thomas. 2000. Reading in the Content Areas: Social Constructivist Dimensions. In *Handbook of Reading Research*, *vol. 3*, eds. M. Kamil, P. Mosenthal, P. D. Pearson, and R. Barr. Mahwah, NJ: Lawrence Erlbaum.

Bromley, Karen. 2004. Rethinking Vocabulary Instruction. *The Language and Literacy Spectrum* 14:3–12.

Melville, Herman. 1851. *Moby Dick*. New York: Harper.

Nagy, William, and Richard C. Anderson. 1984. How Many Words Are There in Printed School English? *Reading Research Quarterly* 19 (3): 304–330.

National Governors Association Center for Best Practices and Council of Chief State School Officers. 2010. Common Core Standards. http://www.corestandards.org/the-standards.

Oatley, Keith. 2009. Changing Our Minds. *Greater Good: The Science of a Meaningful Life*, Winter. http://greatergood.berkeley.edu/article/item/chaning_our_minds.

Pinnell, Gay Su. 1988. Success of Children At Risk in a Program that Combines Writing and Reading. *Technical Report No.* 417 (January). Reading and Writing Connections.

Richek, Margaret. 2005. Words Are Wonderful: Interactive, Time-Efficient Strategies to Teach Meaning Vocabulary. *The Reading Teacher* 58 (5): 414–423.

Riordan, Rick. 2005. *The Lightning Thief*. London: Puffin Books.

Sachar, Louis. 2000. *Holes*. New York, NY: Dell Yearling.

Snicket, Lemony. 1999. *A Series of Unfortunate Events*. New York: HarperCollins.

Tomlinson, Carol Ann and Marcia. B. Imbeau. 2010. *Leading and Managing a Differentiated Classroom*. Alexandria, VA: Association for Supervision and Curriculum Development.

Zunshine, Lisa. 2006. *Why We Read Fiction: Theory of Mind and the Novel*. Columbus, OH: The Ohio State University Press.

Contents of the
Digital Resource CD

Passage	Filename	Pages
Our Little Celtic Cousin of Long Ago	celtic.pdf celtic.doc	31–38
The Store Boy	storeboy.pdf storeboy.doc	39–46
The Rover Boys at School	roverboys.pdf roverboys.doc	47–54
The Prince and the Pauper	prince.pdf prince.doc	55–62
A Little Princess	princess.pdf princess.doc	63–70
Rainbow Valley	rainbow.pdf rainbow.doc	71–78
Little Women	littlewomen.pdf littlewomen.doc	79–86
The Lords of the Wild	lordswild.pdf lordswild.doc	87–94
Kidnapped	kidnapped.pdf kidnapped.doc	95–102
In the Days of the Guild	daysguild.pdf daysguild.doc	103–110
Anne of Green Gables	greengables.pdf greengables.doc	111–118
The Puritan Twins	puritan.pdf puritan.doc	119–126
The Red Badge of Courage	redbadge.pdf redbadge.doc	127–134
The Secret Garden	secretgarden.pdf secretgarden.doc	135–142
The Guns of Bull Run	bullrun.pdf bullrun.doc	143–150